UNEXPECTED VISITORS

"There's no reason to be so rude about this," Clint said as he squared off with his feet shoulder-width apart and his arms relaxed at his sides. "If you've got a legitimate reason to look at Peter's project, then I'm sure he won't have any problem showing it to you."

"We got our reasons for being here that don't concern you."

Turning so that he was looking slightly over his shoulder, but not taking his eyes away from the three intruders, Clint said, "Peter, were you expecting any visitors?"

"No. I wasn't."

"And do you recognize these men as having a good reason to be here and see what you're working on?"

"No. I don't."

Clint held out his hands slightly and shrugged. "There you go, then. It looks like you boys shouldn't be in here after all. I'm going to have to ask you to leave."

The two gunmen at the farthest end of the room started to chuckle. The third, on the other hand, didn't find the situation so amusing.

"And if we don't leave before we get what we came for?" that third man asked.

"Then I hope you came here to be thrown out on your faces," Clint replied without batting an eye. "Because that's all you're going to get . . ."

THE GUNSMITH

262

THE DEVIL'S SPARK

J. R. ROBERTS

JOVE BOOKS, NEW YORK

This is a work of fiction. Names, characters, places, and incidents either
are the product of the author's imagination or are used fictitiously,
and any resemblance to actual persons, living or dead, business
establishments, events, or locales is entirely coincidental.

THE DEVIL'S SPARK

A Jove Book / published by arrangement with
the author

PRINTING HISTORY
Jove edition / October 2003

Copyright © 2003 by Robert J. Randisi

ISBN: 0-515-13625-5

A JOVE BOOK®
Jove Books are published by The Berkley Publishing Group,
a division of Penguin Group (USA) Inc.,
375 Hudson Street, New York, New York 10014.
JOVE and the "J" design
are trademarks belonging to Penguin Group (USA) Inc.

PRINTED IN THE UNITED STATES OF AMERICA

10 9 8 7 6 5 4 3 2 1

ONE

The day felt like cold steel.

Despite the fact that the sun could not be seen, it was still bright enough to see clearly in every direction. What light there was reflected off the thick gray clouds that hung overhead like a cloak. It gave the world a faded quality that seemed reminiscent of a photograph that had been taken long ago.

The trees were still and dead, hardly waving in the wintry breezes that drifted by. Leaves that had once hung from the branches displaying the gold and reds of autumn were now a thick carpet of mulch that stuck to the earth and was worn away bit by bit. It wasn't too cold for that time of year, but it was the kind of chill that felt crisp and refreshing when the wind was low. It was quickly getting colder, however, and would soon become the same kind of chill that could cut through a man's skin with just a little more push of the air.

Much different than the warmer seasons, the cold months had a different kind of peace to them. Sound traveled farther and played easily upon the ears. On cold days, voices seemed to carry greater distances without being disturbed and even the slamming of a door could be heard all the way down at the other end of the street. Much like the feeling of something against a chilled face, sharper

noises acquired even more of a bite and rattled beneath
the gray clouds like a marble in an otherwise empty jar.

The click of metal snapping into place cut through the
air, riding on the heels of the sound of something scraping
against leather. For anyone who'd heard that before, the
sound was unmistakable. Somewhere, a gun had been
drawn from its holster and its hammer had been thumbed
back in preparation to fire.

That sound hadn't gone unnoticed, but there simply
weren't enough people to catch it over the rustle of wagon
wheels, the pounding of horses' hooves, and the squeak-
ing of hinges which filled most towns the size of Gemmell, Idaho. If there had been more folks willing to walk
about in the harsh, early morning chill, the sound might
have drawn more attention. As it was, there were only
two men who heard it.

One of those was the man who'd drawn the gun.

The other stood no more than ten feet away from him,
his eyes glued to the unholstered weapon.

The man holding the pistol kept his hand near his hip
and the barrel pointing forward. His thumb was still resting on the edge of the hammer and his mouth was a
grimly satisfied line. By the looks of him, he could have
been a few years younger than his fifty-four years, which
was mainly due to a narrow, clean-shaven face and a
frame that was still lean and strong. His hands were as
unmoving as the steel he carried and his feet were in a
wide, duelist's stance.

The gun seemed perfectly at home in the man's grasp,
even though he was dressed more as a businessman rather
than the sort who would normally brandish a firearm.
Neatly combed hair was only slightly more gray than
black and was just thin enough to reveal hints of the scalp
underneath.

Standing that all-too-short distance away from the man
with the salt-and-pepper hair was the unarmed fellow who
was obviously several decades the first man's junior. He

stood unmoving as well, but his hands clenched and opened anxiously at his sides.

Swallowing, the younger man let out a breath which turned to steam the moment it passed his lips. He seemed to be transfixed by the weapon held by the person in front of him. Only after a few slow seconds ticked by did he move his eyes away from that gun and look up into the face a few feet above it.

The older man met the other's gaze for a split-second before squeezing the trigger and sending a single shot through the air. Smoke and sparks erupted from the barrel and the thunder which followed blasted apart the cold silence before charging off into the distance.

Even though he'd been expecting the shot, the younger man twitched anyway. His eyes widened and he took half a step back as the smoke and noise washed over him.

Having made a point to keep his eyes focused on the younger man, the gunman turned his attention to the straw-covered alley directly in front of him. At the end of that alley was a row of three boards, only one of which had a paper bull's-eye tacked to its center.

Nodding appreciatively, the younger man grinned and stepped forward. He covered the distance between himself and the older man in a few anxious steps. The alley was almost wide enough to be considered more of a lot and there was enough space for a couple more people to have shared the room. But there was only the two of them, so the sound of his clapping echoed nearly as much as the gunshot.

"I'll be damned," the younger man said. "That's something I didn't think I'd hear for a long time."

Bowing his head slightly, the older man spoke with a voice tinted by a distinctly British accent. "And I thought you were praising that fine display of marksmanship."

The younger man took a quick look down to the other end of the alley, squinted and took another look. His smile grew even wider when he saw that the paper target down there was marred by a single blackened hole which had

been punched directly through the middle of the bull's-
eye. I'll be damned again! That's a hell of a shot, Peter."

"I do get my fair share of practice, but yes. It was
indeed a hell of a shot."

Now that he felt as though he'd been properly acknowl-
edged, the older man faced the younger one. He spun the
pistol around his finger in a tightly controlled motion so
that the weapon wound up with its handle pointing outward. "Care to examine it for yourself?" he asked.

The other man took the gun that was offered to him
and held it on its side in both hands. Gazing down at the
polished steel, he shook his head and let out a low whistle.
"If I didn't know any better, I'd say you scrapped that old
one I gave to you and bought a new one."

"I admit that would have been less expensive."

"But that wouldn't have been the gun my daddy carried
at Shiloh. This one is."

Now both of them were gazing down at the weapon.
The sound of the shot that had been fired had just faded
away completely, but the smell of burnt powder still hung
in the air around them.

TWO

"I didn't think you could do it, Peter," the younger man said. "I honestly didn't."

Flinching at the offhanded way his name was cut short, the older man kept his preferences to himself and turned to walk back toward the nearby door which was held partially open. He kicked away the wooden wedge which held it open and motioned for the younger man to step inside. "Sorry to disappoint you, Benjamin. But that is most definitely your father's gun and you most definitely owe me for services rendered."

Ben laughed to himself and slipped the gun beneath his belt. "I know I gave you a hard time before, but I've heard plenty men say they could fix this firearm only to hand it back a day or two later."

They stepped into a good-sized workshop that smelled like the oiled innards of a gun. There were benches lining two walls and shelves with supplies and tools of all shapes and sizes hanging from every available space. There was even a small blacksmithing area next to a stack of molds that had all been crafted by the same set of hands that had put that bullet through the middle of the bull's-eye.

Leading the way through the workshop and into a smaller room filled with racks and glass cases brimming with pistols and rifles of nearly every make and model, the older man said. "Don't feel too badly. I guarantee all of my work. Besides, you might not be smiling after you see this." Keeping his own face as passive as possible, the older man handed over a folded slip of paper.

This time, it was Ben who flinched. "Damn, that's a pretty penny. But it's worth it to have this gun of mine looking good as new and firing again. I can only pay a piece of this now, though. You want me to leave the gun here until I can scrape together the rest?"

"That won't be necessary, Benjamin," he said as the front door to the shop was opened by another customer. "I know you're good for it."

"Are you sure?"

"You and your family have only lived here as long as I have. In fact, I'll even accept credit at your establishment for some of my payment. That way, I might actually come out ahead in the game."

The customer who'd entered the store was still standing at the doorway behind Benjamin. He let the door swing shut before stepping closer to the pair. "Still scaring your customers by taking them out back?" the newest arrival asked.

Benjamin spun around and took a look at the third man who filled up a good portion of the doorway. The remnants of a smile still hung on his face, even though he didn't quite know what to make of the unfamiliar figure.

"Don't let the English accent fool you," the stranger said. "He's got gunpowder in his blood and the devil's spark in his eye."

Those words obviously confused Benjamin, but struck a definite chord within the older man. Placing his hand on the glass top of a counter as he walked by, the older man stepped around Benjamin so he could get an unimpeded look at who had just stepped through his door. When he saw the stranger's face, he straightened up and let out a single laugh that filled the entire showroom.

"Clint Adams! Is that really you?"

"It sure is, Peter. How have you been?"

Still slightly wary, Benjamin stepped to one side and shifted his eyes between the other two men. "You men know each other?"

"Most definitely, Benjamin, most definitely. Mister Adams here is an acquaintance from some time ago. I scarcely thought he would even remember me after so many years."

"How could I forget someone who can strip down a Peacemaker and fit it back together two seconds faster than me?"

"I believe you meant to say three seconds faster."

Clint tilted his head and narrowed his eyes, making it obvious that he wasn't about to concede his point. The smile that returned to his face, however, made it plain to see that he wasn't about to be mean about it either. "I still say you fixed that watch somehow, but I'll let it slide this time."

Clint stepped forward and clasped the older man's hand so he could shake it vigorously. He then stepped aside when he realized he'd walked right between Peter and his customer. "Sorry for the interruption," Clint said, "but I know this one's tricks. Did he try to scare you by testing out your pistol there?"

"Well, I guess he—"

"I did nothing of the sort," Peter interrupted. "Just demonstrating the quality of my work."

"And the quality of your aim," Clint said with a short jab of his elbow. "How else do you keep everyone in line so well?"

"I swear, you Americans think about nothing but violence. Even when you joke, it's about such crass things as threats and gunplay." When Peter spoke, his accent seemed to thicken. Turning so that he was looking directly at Benjamin, he pocketed the money he'd been given and said, "This will do just fine. As for the rest, you can make it up to me as per the method I suggested. Is that all right?"

"That'll be just fine," Benjamin said, happy to be back

on a subject he fully understood "If I can scrape together enough cash to settle up any sooner, I'll be sure to run it over here to you."

Bowing his head, Peter replied, "Done. It's been a pleasure doing business with you."

The younger man tipped his hat and looked over to Clint. "Nice to meet you as well," he said.

Clint returned the gesture. "Likewise."

Waiting until Benjamin had left the store and closed the door behind him, Peter let out a gruff breath and swatted Clint on the shoulder. "Always showing up at the worst time."

"What's that supposed to mean? I haven't seen you for ten years."

"Twelve is more like it. And that wasn't any better of a time than this. You damn near cost me a sale, just now."

"Oh, stop your whining you old limey and buy me some lunch. I'm starving."

Peter smiled and shook his head. "If memory serves me correctly, you are always starving." He stopped and looked at Clint once more. "It truly is good to see you."

"Same here, Peter." Clint looked around the showroom, taking in the sight of all the different weapons displayed inside the cases and hanging along the wall. "You seem to be doing well for yourself. This place sure beats the hell out of the setup you used to have when I last saw you."

"It had better. That last store was half the size and I didn't even have a workshop. If your memory was better, you'd also recall that previous store was on the other side of town."

"There's nothing wrong with my memory," Clint answered. "I got to town almost half an hour ago and headed to that old store right away. After wandering around like a fool and asking someone, I finally made my way here. Now that I finally arrived, how about a tour?"

"There will be plenty of time for that after we eat. Just seeing you again reminds me of all the steaks and potatoes you tossed down into that gullet of yours. My breakfast of tea and biscuits just doesn't stack up to that."

"Lead the way," Clint said, patting his belly. "Just be sure to take me somewhere that serves strong coffee."

"Not only is the coffee strong, but it is free as well. I've recently made an arrangement with the owner of the finest restaurant in town." Peter took a waistcoat from the hook behind Clint and pulled it on over his lean frame. Before he stepped out through the front door, he took one more look at his visitor and said, "We have a lot of catching up to do."

THREE

If someone had been sitting in a place like San Francisco or London, they might have expected something a little more extravagant from the best restaurant in town. For a town the size of Gemmell, Idaho, the Gemmell Lodge was just extravagant enough to fit the bill.

Clean and big enough to fit over a dozen tables in the main dining room, the Lodge smelled like a mother's kitchen which was more than enough to please Clint's nose. Going by the look on the Englishman's face, Peter was more than a little pleased himself.

Peter and Clint sat at a table in the middle of the room closer to the back. Several picture windows covered the front wall, giving everyone inside a generous view of the town's main street. It wasn't too crowded inside the place, but it was crowded enough for them to feel lucky to get as good a choice of seats as they did.

"I apologize for the table," Peter said. "I know you don't fancy sitting this close to the windows."

Clint rolled his eyes and laughed under his breath. "You know, for someone who makes such a big deal out of not being like the men he sells guns to, you sure do like to act like a gunfighter."

"If I remember correctly, you were the one who made

10

a point to keep your back to a wall during every meal we shared last time."

"Yeah? Well maybe that was because of the outlaws that were gunning for both of our hides at that time. Do you happen to recall that little bit of information?"

"How could I forget?" Peter paused for a second, propped both elbows upon the table and shot a vaguely annoyed smile over toward Clint. "Something I would have been more than happy to forget is that damned rubbish about the devil's spark. How do you bear to hold onto such nonsense for so long?"

Clint let out a short laugh and leaned back in his chair. "Now why would I ever forget something that embarrassed you so badly? I'm just glad to see it hasn't lost its effect on you."

Just then, a portly man dressed in a white shirt and black pants made his way to the table. He looked to Peter and said, "Benny just came by and told me that your money wasn't good here any more. At least for a while anyway."

"In that case," Peter said, "be sure to put this one's meal on my bill as well."

"Sure thing, Mister Banks. What can I get for you two?"

Before Clint could say a word, Peter spoke up. "Two of the specials and a pot of coffee."

"Be right up," the waiter said. "I'll be right back with that coffee."

Clint waited for the waiter to leave before he asked, "What's the special here?"

"Just what you like. Enough meat and bread to choke a racehorse."

"Ah, yes. You remembered."

"Actually, it's a ham steak, three eggs, sliced potatoes, and biscuits. I expect you'll have to help me with mine as well."

"Perfect." Clint was getting hungrier by the second and was glad the waiter was back in no time with the coffee.

The thick brown liquid was steaming hot and smelled as though it had been brewed less than a minute ago. One sip was enough to take some of the chill out of him that had soaked all the way down to his bones after the morning's ride. Another sip and he was able to feel his toes moving inside his boots again.

"So, what brings you around here again, Clint? After the last time we met, I'd have thought you would steer clear of me for the rest of your days."

"Last time might have gotten a little dicey," Clint said. "But I've had a whole lot worse. Actually, I found myself over in Montana and thought I'd head over this way to pay you a visit."

"Still wandering wherever the winds carry you? After staying put all this time, I'm truly envious."

"Looks like you've done well enough for yourself, Peter. I'm actually surprised you haven't moved to a bigger town or even someplace like California or Colorado. There's always a call for craftsmen like you and in those places, you'd make a hell of a lot more money."

"I entertained the notion of packing up and moving to Dodge City at the suggestion of a lawman who passed through here some time ago. But then I found out that he only suggested Dodge because of its rather notorious reputation."

Smirking, Clint said, "I've heard Dodge called a whole lot worse, but I'd say that you've got it more or less right. Still, you wouldn't have to wait more than an hour or two between jobs out there, I'd wager."

"I'm sure. But they would have been jobs working for the wrong type of people."

"People who need to hire a gunsmith usually are the same ones that use guns, Peter. There's just not a lot of ways around that."

Peter sipped his coffee with the slow precision he might have reserved for high tea back in his native Manchester. After letting the hot liquid warm his mouth and ease down his throat, he nodded once to the words Clint had spoken.

"True enough. Perhaps Dodge is just a little too rowdy for me all the same. Come to think of it, I'm surprised you never set up a shop of your own. You always had some measure of skill in the trade."

"Some measure?" Clint asked, mimicking Peter's accent. "I'm not too far away from your league and don't you forget it."

"Only after I taught you nearly all of my tricks, boyo. And don't you forget that. Even when we were taking contracts within a few miles of each other, the most generous of testimonials put you as second to my first."

Clint held up both hands and nodded. "You got me there. I just wonder why you paid such close attention to what I taught you if you were just going to use those lessons to show off when testing your merchandise."

"You should know better than that, Clint. I wanted to learn to shoot better so I could get a better feel for my own craft. Otherwise, I'd be like a cook who never bothers to sample his own food." Suddenly, his eyes lit up and he leaned forward. The expression on his face resembled that of a kid getting a look at his Christmas presents. "Speaking of my craft. Excuse me," Peter said, cutting himself off. "Our craft. Speaking of which, I'd very much like to see that fine piece of yours you were so very proud of."

Acting offended, Clint said, "You act like I shouldn't be proud. That was a damn fine piece of work. It still is!"

"And I would never imply otherwise. Just let me get a look before you get your delicate sensibilities all twisted into a knot."

Unable to maintain his act for more than a few seconds, Clint pushed back a bit from the table and drew the Colt from its holster at his side. He caught the attention of nearly everyone around him, but didn't let the nervous stares get to him. Instead, he set the Colt down onto the table and slid it over to Peter.

As soon as they saw the Englishman pick up the

weapon and start examining it, the rest of the diners relaxed and went back to their own plates.

Peter turned the Colt over in his hands and looked over
every inch with a slow, expert stare. He nodded, opened
the cylinder and turned the mechanism so he could carefully listen to each individual click. Snapping it shut with
a flick of his wrist, he gently handed the weapon back to
its owner.

"A bit outdated, but it was good enough in its day, I
suppose," Peter finally said.

Clint's face dropped. "What? Outdated?"

After holding on to his straight face for record time,
Peter allowed his grin to break through. "I'm glad to see
I can still pull one over on you as well every now and
then."

Before Clint had a chance to fire back, the waiter had
returned with their food.

FOUR

Clint didn't realize just how hungry he was until he'd put that first bit of ham into his mouth. As soon as the food hit his tongue, it was all he could do to keep himself from inhaling the rest. The breakfast would have been great under any circumstances, but after eating rations, jerky, and beans for the last few days, it was positively inspirational.

As he ate, he listened to Peter talk about how he'd spent the last several years. As good a friend as he considered the Englishman to be, Clint was in no way enthralled by the gunsmith's work stories, which ranged from one fairly interesting assignment to another.

They were fairly interesting by Peter's standards, anyway.

Clint did his best to nod when it was appropriate and try not to look too bored as he finished every last bit of his meal. As promised, he was given a good portion of Peter's plate as well.

"Are you about ready to come up for air?" Peter asked. "Or should I drone on about my uninteresting career some more?"

Clint nearly choked on the food in his mouth. Quickly swallowing and clearing his throat, he dabbed at his

15

mouth with a napkin before saying, "Not at all, Peter. I
don't mind hearing about all of this."

"Really? Then tell me the make of the gun I was just
talking about."

Clint scoffed as though the question was so easy it was
absurd. When he opened his mouth to answer, however,
there was nothing ready to come out. He held up his finger
and thought for a moment, but try as he might, he couldn't
remember anything except for what was filling his stomach.

"All right, all right," Clint groaned. "I'm sorry."

Peter waved away the apology. "Not at all. I was barely
paying attention to myself. I just don't like to eat in silence. It's not civilized to have a meal with friends and
not converse."

"I don't know. A quiet meal is always welcome when
I'm around."

"If you want to call me a dull bag of wind, just come
out with it, Clint."

"You know that's not what I—"

"I know. But now that I have both of our attention,
there's something I would like to talk about. In fact, I'm
even more glad that you're here since I doubt anyone else
could quite share my excitement."

For the first time since the plate had been put in front
of him, Clint forgot about the delicious meal. "All right.
Now you've got my interest. What's got you so worked
up?"

For a moment, it seemed as though something was
wrong. In fact, there was nothing truly wrong with Peter.
It was simply that Clint had never seen such a delighted
grin on the Englishman's face. The smile was so wide
that it was out of character for someone who normally did
his best to always keep his chin up and his stature in tact.

Taking a quick breath, Peter looked as though he was
about to burst. "I just received a contract. Actually, it was
a little under a week ago. It was initially for a series commissioned by the United States Army, but it has since

turned into something much more than that."

"The army? How did someone from the military find you all the way out here?"

"Word of mouth, my good man," Peter replied, putting on a bit more of a showy air. "It travels almost as much as the rumors that I hear concerning your particular exploits."

"Point taken. Go on."

Peter started to continue with his story, but stopped himself before getting another word out. He leaned forward and stared directly into Clint's eyes as he spoke in a quieter voice. "A man contacted me who I knew as an armorer for the U.S. Cavalry. Since then, he's moved on to bigger and better things and has since become a man of very good standing."

"You know him from before?"

"Only slightly," Peter answered with a shrug. "Our paths crossed only professionally when I was still working back east. He admired a rifle I was fitting for a sharpshooter who'd lost a finger and told me he did some work for the government. Every so often since then, I've gotten a contract here and there from him which has been more than enough to see me through the leaner times of my career."

Clint listened carefully to every word the Englishman said. He'd known Peter for some time and had him to thank for many of his own gunsmithing techniques, but he'd never known all of this. In a way, he was surprised at himself for not figuring Peter was taking jobs from other sources. After all, how else was an expert in his field going to make a living in such a small town as Gemmell, Idaho?

"What kind of contracts did you get from the military?" Clint asked.

Pausing for a moment to think it over, Peter shrugged and said, "A dozen or so. Mostly they were modifications to existing weapons, fitting them to perform better under harsh conditions. A soldier in the field rarely has time to properly care for his equipment, you know."

"I guess." Clint stopped himself before asking for Peter
to expand what he'd said. The only reason for that was
because he knew only too well the Englishman would go
into excruciating detail about every last technical detail
until even Clint himself was lost in the flood of information. Besides, those past jobs interested him less than
whatever it was that had gotten Peter so excited right now,
which was exactly what Clint told him.

Leaning in again and fixing his eyes on Clint, Peter
said, "I'm glad you asked about that. You know how I
get started. It's just so rare that I get a chance to talk to
someone who understands what I have to say on this matter. I sometimes doubt that my friend in the military even
knows all the subtleties of firearm manufacture."

Clint had to smile at the way Peter reacted to talking
about guns. It reminded him of a child describing his favorite bedtime story. "I doubt anyone knows those subtleties as well as you do. So are you going to tell me
about this new project or am I supposed to guess?"

"Are you familiar with the Gatling gun?"

Just hearing that name put a picture into Clint's mind
of a soldier crouched behind the enormous weapon which
resembled a half-dozen long rifle barrels connected by a
steel frame and put into a circle. By simply turning a
crank on the side of the gun, that soldier could pump out
a hail storm of hot lead as the barrels turned and bullets
were spat out. He'd only seen one in action a few times
and none of them had been pleasant.

Nodding slightly, Clint said, "I've seen a Gatling or
two."

Peter didn't respond to the dark look on Clint's face at
all. In fact, he spoke with animated enthusiasm since he
viewed weapons as works of mechanical art rather than
anything destructive. Not that the Englishman had any
delusions about what his creations were used for, but Peter
simply figured that he was providing a necessary service
so long as he was careful to provide it to the right people.

That was the reason Peter didn't want to live in Dodge City or some other such "notorious" place.

"If you're familiar with a Gatling, than you can truly appreciate what I've been commissioned to do," Peter went on. "You see, it's partly . . ." He drifted off just then as he sat back and threw the napkin that had been on his lap onto the table. "You know what? Rather than talk any more, why don't I show you what I'm working on?"

"You have a working model?" Clint asked, his curiosity piqued.

"Not quite perfect, but it's enough to show you the concept of what it is I'm working on." And with that, Peter was off of his chair and heading for the door.

It was all Clint could do to keep up with him as the Englishman left the restaurant.

FIVE

Instead of a bill for the food, all Clint and Peter got was a farewell wave from the waiter. After a meal as big and tasty as the breakfast he'd had, Clint thought he might be in the wrong line of work. Perhaps he should live up to his name a little more often if that meant eating like a king without having to go near his money.

Clint needed every bit of strength he'd gotten from the hearty breakfast just to keep up with Peter as he bolted through the front door and walked briskly down the street. The Englishman spoke with wide, fast gestures and somehow managed to keep his voice down to an excited whisper to protect the secrecy of his project.

It struck Clint as somewhat amusing just how careful Peter was being when nobody but an experienced gunsmith would have been able to understand what the hell Peter was saying in the first place. As he went on about muzzle velocities, powder ratios, and barrel temperatures, Peter glanced nervously at every face around as if he thought the locals had all become experts in his field.

Peter was in no danger of breaking his stride, so Clint let him go at full speed while whispering the entire way. Many could rightfully consider Clint an expert in the smithing of firearms, and yet some of what Peter was talking about managed to fly over his head as well.

Knowing the Englishman as well as he did, Clint merely nodded whether he truly understood or not, certain that all would be explained in time. Of course, getting a look at what all this fuss was about would go a long way in helping him clear those things up.

They started off heading toward Peter's shop. Clint recognized the streets well enough since they were simply backtracking over the path they'd taken to get their breakfast. Right before the storefront came into view, Peter turned sharply and nearly left Clint behind.

It took a moment for Clint to realize that he was still going one way and Peter was suddenly headed in another. But all he had to do was catch that incessant whispering for him to know that the source of the chatter was no longer directly beside him. Clint turned on the balls of his feet and adjusted his speed so he could catch up to Peter who was still going on about reloading speed ratios as though Clint hadn't missed a word.

Peter turned sharply once again, leading both of them down a narrow alley.

"Do you have this project of yours someplace special?" Clint asked.

Pausing for a split second, Peter shook his head. "No, not at all. I'm merely using the rear entrance to my shop. You never know when someone might be keeping an eye on you during a project like this."

"Do you get followed a lot when working on these secret contracts?"

"Not a lot. Sometimes, but not a lot."

Clint had been comforted by the first part of that answer. The second part, on the other hand, had much the opposite effect.

But Peter had already pulled himself back onto his own conversational track and was just breaching the subject of various types of coolants when he started digging in his pocket for his keys. Clint kept one ear on what his friend was saying and the rest of his senses looking out for a suspicious face or figure lurking in the shadows.

There were no faces to be seen, however, and the sun had broken through the clouds to chase away most of the shadows. Even so, Clint found his stomach tightening around the food he'd just eaten. He couldn't quite put his finger on a source for his concerns, but they were still there, nonetheless.

"Believe me when I tell you," Peter said as he got closer to the tall wooden fence that enclosed his little private shooting range. "This is going to take your breath away when you see this. It's not completely my own design, but I've managed to carry it a long way since it was entrusted to my care."

"I can't wait," Clint said, his eyes still searching the alley on every side. At that moment, a noise caught his ear. It sounded as though someone might be walking along a rooftop or might have tripped over a stray piece of lumber lying on the ground.

Clint's nerves settled immediately when he saw what had caused the noise. In fact, he felt more than a little foolish when he saw that it had only been Peter fidgeting with the wooden latch on the gate of his back lot.

Oblivious to all of Clint's reservations, Peter finally managed to get the gate open and push the door aside. "I'm not accustomed to entering this way," he said with a shrug. "Normally I just keep this gate locked, altogether."

The Englishman's eyes narrowed slightly and he studied Clint's face. "Are you quite all right? You look a bit pale."

"Apart from being taken for a run right after I finished eating, I'm doing just fine."

"I have been a most atrocious host, haven't I? Well, with the credit I have around town, I'll be able to make it up to you. One of the owners of the town's biggest saloon still owes me for a job as well. He's more than anxious to pay me back with credit at one of his gaming tables. Perhaps you'd have better luck there than I would."

"All right, Peter," Clint said, shaking his head. "Can

we just get inside before my fingers start to go numb? It's starting to snow."

Peter looked up and smiled. "So it is. An even better omen." Both men were inside the lot behind Peter's shop and they reflexively quickened their steps as they crossed the space used for test-firing weapons. There was something about being that close to a pistol target that tended to make any man a little nervous.

From there, Peter headed for the back door to his shop and singled out the proper key on his ring. He fit the key into the lock, turned it, and then pushed the door open with building excitement. As soon as he took another step inside, Peter froze.

Clint stepped in behind him and nearly ran into the Englishman's back. Before he could ask what the problem was, Clint spotted several figures moving through the workshop headed in his direction.

"Good to see you, Peter," one of the figures said. "Maybe you can tell us where that fancy gun is so we don't have to tear this place apart."

SIX

Clint knew there was someone in the room before he'd even stepped all the way inside. It had been more on the instinctual level, but when he saw the men standing there, he found that he wasn't in the least bit surprised.

There were three of them in all. Two stood at the opposite end of the room from where Peter was standing with one on either side of the door leading to the showroom. The third man was the one who'd just spoken and he was walking straight through the workshop, making a direct line toward Peter.

All of them wore holsters around their waists and had a hand resting on the grip of their weapon.

"You gonna save us some time and effort and tell us where this thing is?" the third gunman asked. "Or are you gonna force us to make you talk through a mouth of broken teeth?"

Hearing that, Clint stepped out from behind his friend and positioned himself slightly in front of Peter.

The gunman in the middle of the group was obviously the leader of the bunch since he kept the other two back with a casual gesture from his free hand. "Well, who is this?" he asked, looking at Clint. "Another one of your English friends here to swap spit and jaw about the Queen?"

The other two intruders seemed to find that amusing and chuckled under their breath.

Clint smirked as well, putting the trio at ease just enough for him to close a bit more distance before anyone got too nervous. "If you're here to see what Peter is working on, you're going to have to stand in line."

"We don't stand in no lines, mister. And just because we don't know your name doesn't mean we won't put you on your ass just as fast as we'll put down this limey asshole."

"There's no reason to be so rude about this," Clint said as he squared off with his feet shoulder-width apart and his arms relaxed at his sides. "If you've got a legitimate reason to look at Peter's project, then I'm sure he won't have any problem showing it to you."

"We got our reasons for being here that don't concern you."

Turning so that he was looking slightly over his shoulder, but not taking his eyes away from the three intruders, Clint said, "Peter, were you expecting any visitors?"

The Englishman didn't sound overly aggressive, but he hadn't backed down an inch yet, either. "No," he said to Clint. "I wasn't."

"And do you recognize these men as having a good reason to be here and see what you're working on?"

"No. I don't."

Shaking his head, Clint turned so that he was once again staring straight into the faces of the three men standing before him. He held out his hands slightly and shrugged. "There you go, then. It looks like you boys shouldn't be in here after all. I'm going to have to ask you to leave."

Once again, the two gunmen at the farthest end of the room started to chuckle. The third, on the other hand, didn't find the situation so amusing.

"And what if we don't leave before we get what we came here for?" that third man asked.

"Then I hope you came here to be thrown out on your

faces," Clint replied without batting an eye. "Because that's all you're going to get."

Reflexively, the two at the other end of the room started moving forward. The expressions on their faces were those of dogs who'd just gotten their supper ripped from between their jaws. Once they got a little closer, Clint could tell the men were fairly large and oafish. They struck him as the types who would club a man with their pistols rather than pull the triggers.

The third man was leaner and more aware, however, and didn't take the bait that Clint had dangled in front of them. "Hold it," he said, without looking behind him.

He didn't have to look to know that the other two would follow his command. They both stopped as if they'd reached the end of their leashes.

"Who the hell are you?" the third gunman asked.

Clint glared across with enough intensity to start a fire. "I'm the man asking you politely to leave."

The leader of the trio cocked his head to one side and took a moment to let the everything soak in. He looked over to Peter and then smirked ever so slightly. If a wolf or a shark could smile, it might have looked an awful lot like the grimace worn by the gunman at that moment.

It was that same moment when Clint knew the talking was over.

SEVEN

Having been through the almost ritualistic path that lead up to a gunfight, Clint was steeling himself for what he knew to be coming. He could feel the tensions escalating right up to the certain explosion that could come at any second.

He didn't know exactly when it would happen, but he knew for certain that one of those three would lose his patience and make a stupid move that would light the fuse on the whole situation. There was only so much talking that could be done and if these other men could be turned back with words alone, Clint would have done it by now.

But whoever those men were, Clint could tell they weren't there to talk. They wanted to get their hands on Peter's project one way or another and weren't about to leave one second before that goal was realized.

Clint's muscles tensed and his body coiled like a spring. He figured one of the other two men would make his move before their leader. That third one just seemed to have a little too much experience to fly off the handle so quickly. All the same, Clint wasn't about to take his eyes off of either of them. Every time his gaze darted between one man and another, he could feel himself tensing up even more.

The room was quiet as a tomb, yet bristling with activity.

It felt like the prickly, invisible fingers which ran over a man's skin just before a storm broke.

"Hold it!"

Those two words came so suddenly, that they were nearly enough to push everyone else over the edge. The two gunmen on either side of the third came closest to jumping the gun, but barely managed to keep themselves from doing anything that would start the lead flying.

It was Peter who'd broken the silence. He stepped to one side, moving toward the wall with his hands held out in front of him.

"I don't want this to happen like this," the Englishman said. "Just let me see if I can accommodate you fellows."

Clint glanced quickly over to him, not quite believing what he was hearing. "Are you sure about this?"

Peter shook his head so slightly that Clint himself barely noticed. "Just let me get the plans for the cannon," he said. "Then we can finish this properly."

Clint watched as Peter moved toward a chest that was sitting against the wall. The three gunmen were watching as well, but didn't seem as close to firing their weapons as they had been a moment ago.

"Good choice, Peter," the leader of the intruders said. "Maybe you're not as dumb as your friend here."

Positioning himself so he could keep tabs on all four of the other men in the room, Clint wondered if Peter was really about to hand over the project he'd been so secretive about mere minutes ago. With that in mind, Clint's mind filled up with all the things Peter had been saying on the way over to the shop from the restaurant.

According to the older gunsmith, this weapon was something he didn't even want someone to hear about accidentally. He'd talked about so many facts and figures that even though Clint hadn't been paying attention to every bit of it, he was still impressed by the bits he did manage to catch.

Suddenly, Clint's mind focused in on one particular thing.

Peter had talked about Gatling guns, barrel-to-powder ratios, and everything under the sun. Everything, that is, except for cannons. Not once had Peter said anything that led Clint to think he was working on anything close to a cannon.

When Clint took another look at the chest that Peter was opening, he could see that only the smallest cannon parts could even fit in a container of that size.

There was no cannon.

Peter had only used that word as a way to tip off Clint. Luckily, Clint had figured it out with about a second and a half to spare.

Peter was doing a good job of keeping his cards covered. If not for the one-word hint he'd dropped, Clint doubted that even he would have guessed anything was amiss until it was too late. And now that the moment was here, he could only roll with it and hope for the best.

"Hurry it up," the lead intruder grunted. "We don't have all damn day."

Peter's hand disappeared into the chest for no more than half a second. After that, he straightened up and pulled the .44 revolver from where it had been stashed.

The instant the Englishman tipped his hand and brought his weapon into the open, all three intruders sprung to action. The leader of the group demonstrated his experience by dropping to one knee before firing, making himself the smallest target of the three.

Although the other two weren't levelheaded enough to know they should take some defensive action, they made up for it in their desire to draw blood. Both of them raised their weapons and squeezed their triggers, taking hasty shots in the general direction of Clint and Peter's side of the room.

Clint was more than ready to go and took his shot at the same time as Peter. The shots fired at them missed by several feet, neither of which caused either man to do

more than flinch as the rounds hissed by. Both the .44
and Clint's Colt roared simultaneously, filling the workshop with smoke and thunder as lead was spit through the
air toward the intruders.

Clint's shot caught the gunman who was standing closest to him. It happened to be one of the men who had
already fired and the bullet spun him in a tight circle as
it tore a path through his upper body. Clint couldn't tell
exactly where he'd hit the other man and wasn't about to
check. All he knew was that the man was on his way
down to the floor and that was good enough for the moment.

Peter had instinctually shot at the gunman who'd fired
at him and was quick enough to hit his mark before the
other man dove for cover. The expression on the Englishman's face was calm and determined, even as he pulled
the trigger. His aim was good enough so that even though
the gunman had been dropping to the floor, he was
wounded by the time he got there.

The leader of the three didn't take the time to look at
either of his men. Instead, he was drawing his gun and
lining up his shot. By the time everyone else had fired,
he'd had enough time to aim and pull his own trigger.

Clint had been watching that third man the entire time.
Since he was working on the adrenaline that surged
through his body, he had enough time to take another shot
before Peter's target hit the floor. Rather than put another
round into either of the other two gunmen, Clint shifted
his aim toward the one in the middle.

Handling the Colt as if it was an extension of his own
hand, Clint pointed it toward where he wanted the lead to
go and fired. It sounded as though the sound of his shot
was somehow drawn out in the ruckus, but that was only
because the third gunman had fired as well. Clint's round
was just punching into the third gunman's ribs as that man
was taking his shot.

When the leader of the intruders pulled his trigger, his
aim was thrown off by the impact of the bullet which

chewed into his flesh. Pain lanced through his entire body and the gun roared in his hand.

Peter clenched his teeth and dropped to the floor as hot metal drilled into his body.

All Clint remembered about that moment was spotting Peter dropping to the floor out of the corner of his eye.

EIGHT

"Peter," Clint said as he rushed to the fallen Englishman's side. "Are you all right?"

Peter tried to speak, but all that came out was a labored croaking sound. Then, his eyes widened and he twisted his body in what looked like a painful spasm. Once he was turned so that his shoulders were both pressed against the wall, Peter raised his right hand and brought his gun up to bear.

Clint hardly even noticed the firearm in the other man's fist. He noticed it well enough once it went off and nearly blinded him with a sudden, fiery splash of smoke and sparks. His instinct was to return fire, but that was choked back almost immediately once his brain reminded his reflexes who he'd be shooting at.

The bullet whipped past Clint's head like an angry wasp, slicing through the air and then punching through the skull of the gunman Clint had wounded only moments ago.

The gunman closest to Clint had been shot through the torso, but had apparently had enough steam left in him to try and fire off a round of his own. He'd gotten as far as lifting his gun and tightening his finger around the trigger before Peter's bullet had put his lights out for good.

Once he saw that he'd dropped his target, Peter allowed

himself to fall back against the wall and let out a painful
breath. "I'll live, Clint," he said. "Just make sure you do
the same."

Nodding, Clint said, "Sit tight. I'll be right back."

Clint could sense the third man taking aim at him without having to see anything. The impending danger hung
over him like a cloud which announced its presence simply by blotting out the sun. Allowing his reflexes to carry
him through the rest of the way, Clint straightened his
arm and took a shot at the last spot where he'd seen that
gunman kneeling on the floor.

It wasn't quite as impressive as Wild Bill hitting a
matchstick by firing over his shoulder with the help of a
hand mirror, but Clint's little trick got the job done. His
Colt barked once again and sent a bullet toward the leader
of the intruders a split second before that man took one
more shot at him.

Just as he'd known to get down before the shooting
started, that gunman also knew better than to stay in that
same position once the fight was under way. He'd shifted
a couple steps to his left, which was the only thing that
saved him from getting a fresh hole blown through his
skull. Clint's round sliced a shallow trench through his
scalp and started a ringing in his head that made the whole
world spin around him.

Clint stood back up to his full height and held his gun
at his hip. The blood was pounding through him and yet
he still managed to keep himself from being carried away
by it. His eyes snapped from one side of the room to
another, taking a quick inventory of what threats remained.

The gunman closest to him was slumped at an awkward
position against the wall. His head was cracked open like
an egg and leaking its contents onto the floor, so there
was no doubt that he was out of the game. That left two
others to contend with. The shooter who'd been standing
against the wall closest to Peter was gripping a bloody
wound in his lower abdomen and struggling to get his

wits about him. The man in the middle was shaking his
head and had dropped to his knees like a drunk who'd
gone way past his limit.

Clint stepped forward and made his way toward both
of the remaining men. While walking around the leader
of the trio, Clint swept a foot out and disarmed that man
with a sharp, swift kick. Another backward swing of the
same leg knocked out the arm the third man had been
using for support, which dropped that gunman flat on his
face.

"Set the pistol down," Clint said to the shooter who
had finally managed to stand up using the wall for support. "And I'd do it real slow if I were you. Both of us
are a little jumpy right now."

It was obvious from the first time that man had made
his presence known that he wasn't exactly the sharpest
knife in the drawer. He struck Clint as more of a stupid
animal who would choke himself if he was tied up for
too long rather than chew through the rope. Even when
he was no longer on the strongest side of the fight, he still
looked as if he had to think about Clint's proposal.

When the gunman finally did let the pistol drop from
his fingers, it seemed as though he was just tired of thinking about it rather than having come to any kind of decision. The meanness was still fresh on his face, only
strengthened by the pain that stabbed through him from
the wound Peter had given him.

"Now tell me," Clint said, stopping in front of the gunman and keeping well out of arm's reach. "What is this
all about?"

The gunman winced and steeled himself against a fresh
wave of burning pain. "He knows," the man said, nodding
once toward Peter. "Why don't you ask him?"

"Because I'd rather ask you. Now answer me before I
lose my patience."

"Just like we said. We want that gun."

"And how did you know about it?"

Nearby, Clint could hear the sounds of boots and hands

scraping against the floorboards as the trio's leader kept struggling to get to his feet. Clint knew only too well what the other man was fighting through. Even if a bullet doesn't do much damage, having one scrape across your skull is like getting knocked by a rock that was flying faster than the eye could see.

"If you . . . have to ask th . . . that question," the third man stammered. "Then you n . . . need to talk to your friend . . . some more."

Dropping the Colt back into its holster, Clint walked right up to the man with the creased skull and grabbed him by the front of his shirt. He pulled him closer to the other remaining gunman in a swift, half-circle of motion and backed him against the wall.

Although he didn't slam his back against the wooden boards, Clint did shake him a bit in the process. He did that partly to keep both men where he could keep close tabs on them and partly because he knew the motion was disorienting the leader of the intruders that much more.

"One of your men is dead," Clint snarled. "And the only reason you two are still alive is because we're not cold-blooded killers like you. Either one of you starts showing a little gratitude or I might just lose some of my generosity."

NINE

Clint had most definitely succeeded in keeping the man in his grip off balance. That gunman's eyes were wavering in their sockets and unable to focus on any one target. His feet were trying to keep flat against the floor, but if not for Clint holding him up, he would have been flat on his backside.

"Who sent you here?"

He started to speak, but the man Clint was holding up had to clench his mouth shut before his queasiness brought all of his food rushing back up again. After swallowing the stuff that had risen to the back of his throat, the gunman let out a rancid breath and said, "I don't know his name. The others just call him Major."

"Major?" Clint asked. "Like a military major?"

"I guess." He had to choke back another wave of nausea before spitting out the next couple words. "I only seen him once."

"Who are these others you mentioned?"

"The . . . others around him. Hired guns by the look of 'em. I only just started working for the man."

Clint could tell fewer of his words were getting through with every question he asked. Keeping that in mind, he pulled the gunman closer and practically shouted directly into his face. "How many others are there?"

". . . don't know. Six or five or so."

"Well be sure to tell this major of yours that he won't get what he's after. Not while I'm here and not while he tries to send punks like you after my friend."

Grunting occasionally from pain, the other remaining gunman had been making his way around to Clint's side. He might as well have announced his presence with a telegram, because Clint knew he was coming since the other man took his first clumsy step.

Just as the other gunman was about to make his move, Clint twisted his upper body and pitched the leader of the group aside. The dizzy man stumbled a few steps before colliding straight into his companion. It was all the dim-witted thug could do to keep from being knocked over as his leader was tossed into him like a sack of dirty laundry.

Clint was ready to follow up his throw with something else, but there was no need. The dumber of the two gun-men had his hands full trying to keep himself and his boss from toppling over and the leader of the intruders was occupied with swimming through the dizziness that still impeded his vision.

Looking down, Clint noticed that neither of the other men had managed to get to their guns so he let them step away from him and back toward the door from which they'd entered the workshop. There was a grunted con-versation between the two, but most of it was one man asking another if they were all right or not.

Clint listened to what he could and followed the two through Peter's shop. He even held the front door open for them and barely fought back the impulse to give them a gentle kick in the backside on their way out.

As soon as they were on the street again, Clint sprinted back to the workshop where Peter was sitting with his back against one of the benches. "Can you hold out for a little bit?"

The older man sucked in a breath and nodded. "It hurts, but I'll muddle through."

"Good. I want to see if I can follow up a bit more on this and then I'll fetch a doctor."

"What are you aiming to do?" Peter asked.

"I want to catch up to those two I just let go. Hopefully, they'll lead me to a bigger fish."

"Carry on, then. I can make it to the doctor myself."

Clint would have preferred for the Englishman to stay put and wait for help to be brought to him, but he doubted that he had enough time to stand around and debate the issue. Comfortable in the knowledge that Peter's wounds weren't too bad, Clint bolted through the shop once again and headed out the front door.

The last time he'd seen them, Clint had spotted the two remaining intruders limping down the street after turning left from Peter's front door. Sure enough, they hadn't changed direction in the couple seconds since Clint had left them and they didn't have enough wind in their sails to pick up their pace to much more than a slow amble.

In fact, Clint had to keep himself in check before he made too much noise in his haste to catch up with them. His boots nearly made enough noise on the boardwalk to draw unwanted attention to himself. The snow which had just started to fall had already dusted the boardwalk with white powder and caused his feet to slide a bit when he reined himself to a stop.

With his eyes glued to the backs of those wounded men, Clint gave them a little more of a lead and then started walking casually behind them. The guppies didn't seem to know they were leading him upstream and that was just the way Clint liked to fish.

TEN

The air had the crisp stillness that only came with winter and caused all of the nearby sounds to freeze in the air like so much exhaled breath. There were more people about than before breakfast and several of them were glancing with concern over to the pair who were obviously wounded and making their way down the street. The two intruders met every concerned gaze with a rude sneer and kept their heads down while continuing along their way.

All of that made it easier for Clint to fall into step a ways behind the wounded pair and blend into the flow of people walking on one side of the street. His feet crunched in the newly fallen snow and flakes settled upon his face, shoulders, and hat. A shingle hanging from a nearby storefront marked the doctor's office only a few lots away from Peter's place, but the two men had already passed that by and were turning the corner onto James Street.

Clint had only followed the pair for a little over a block before they stepped up to a door which led into a narrow building next to a gambling club. Upon a little closer look, Clint could tell that the narrow building was actually not separate from the gambling house at all, but attached to it. More than likely, it was a cathouse or some small hotel that catered to the card-playing crowd.

Once he saw the two wounded men enter the narrow building and close the door behind them, Clint nodded to himself and turned around. He rubbed his hands together to fight the chill that was creeping under his skin and was taken aback by the sight of a young woman who'd been walking behind him.

"Sorry about that," Clint said with a tip of his hat. "I got a little turned around there."

The woman was an attractive blonde who was wrapped up in a dark blue shawl that matched her thick cotton skirt. She smiled. "That's all right. Too bad you're not headed inside after all," she said, glancing toward the gambling club. "I was just hoping for a new face at the table."

Her eyes were light green and so attractive that Clint could hardly look away from them. "Perhaps I'll change my mind before the day's through. I prefer to do most of my playing at night."

She smiled in a way that made her look anything but innocent. "I know exactly what you mean. My name's Amanda."

"I'm Clint."

"All right, Clint, I'll keep an eye out for you later on, then. If you do change your mind about coming by, be sure to give a little more warning than when you decided to make that about-face just now." And with that, the blonde continued walking to the gambling club.

As much as Clint wanted to watch her go, he only had to think about Peter sitting wounded in his workshop to quicken his steps back in that direction. Now that he didn't have to worry about attracting attention or making noise, he covered the distance to the Englishman's shop in half the time.

Stepping through the door, Clint was expecting to find Peter right where he'd left him. The best he'd been hoping for was that the Englishman was still conscious and not bleeding too badly. Clint hadn't gotten too close a look at his friend's wound, but he was fairly certain it wasn't anything close to serious.

What he hadn't been expecting was to find Peter not only up and on his feet, but almost ready to step through the front door on his own. Because of that, Clint damn near knocked over his second person in as many minutes.

"Jesus, Peter, you startled me," Clint said after coming to a quick, jarring stop.

The Englishman smirked and started to laugh, but gritted his teeth since the movement caused him to irritate his bullet wound. "Sorry to disappoint you, lad, but I did say I'd try to muddle through."

"There's muddling and there's muddling straight through to bleeding out. Are you going to at least let me help you to the doctor's office?"

"If it would make you feel better," Peter said through clenched teeth. "I was rather hoping you'd clean up the mess in my workshop, as well. That bloke won't be getting any fresher."

Clint kept away from the side of Peter's body where his shirt was soaked through with blood. Instead, he put the Englishman's left arm over his shoulder and let Peter lean on him for support. Since he didn't know exactly where the wound was, Clint was reluctant to do anything else unless Peter seemed to need it.

As it was, the older man appeared to be doing well enough on his own. He accepted Clint's help, but didn't lean on him with all of his weight. Even when they went down the steps leading to the street, Clint noticed that Peter was doing a good portion of the walking on his own.

"You're a tough old bird, you know that?" Clint commented as they climbed the few steps leading up to the doctor's office. "I'll bet you could have made it here on your own."

"Is that a polite way to say you're regretting carrying me?"

Clint smiled and reached out to open the doctor's door. "I'm American. We don't have to be polite to you Brits anymore."

"Oh, hell. Here we go again with that nonsense. If you

Yanks would just pay your taxes, we never would have been forced to cut you loose from the U.K." Although he looked awfully tired when he glanced over to meet Clint's gaze, Peter still had the familiar humor in his eye. "But remember, we'll take you back whenever you colonists see the error of your ways."

Both Clint and Peter were inside the doctor's office by now and had been spotted by a burly young man with a head of thick brown hair. His skin was a rich, sandy color and he moved with speed across the room to aid the wounded man leaning against Clint.

"You the doctor?" Clint asked.

"I'm Doctor Garza, yes." Looking to the Englishman, he asked, "What happened to you, Peter?"

"One of us colonists took a shot at him," Clint replied. "Better sew this limey's mouth up while you're at it, Doc, or I might finish the job."

The doctor looked appalled to hear such talk. But Clint was smiling at Peter even as he spoke them and Peter was laughing hard enough to split his side open even more than it already was.

ELEVEN

Doctor Garza had been on the trail ever since he'd come up from Mexico at age seven. He had the thick muscles and tough skin of a hard worker, but still handled Peter even gentler than Clint had been able to no matter how hard he'd tried. The doctor moved Peter over to a bed near the back of his office and immediately began examining the wound.

Peter's shirt was soaked with so much blood that Clint had been expecting to see a much bigger wound once the garment was pulled aside. In fact, after Doctor Garza had washed away some of the blood that had caked onto Peter's skin, it was hard to spot the original wound at all.

"Don't look so disappointed," Peter said to Clint. "It still hurts like a bugger."

Shaking his head, the doctor wrung out his bloody towel and dipped it into a water basin. "Do you two know each other?"

"Pardon my manners, Doctor," Peter said. "This is Clint Adams. He's a colleague of mine from way back."

Doctor Garza smiled and dropped his towel into the basin again. "Well, by the way you two were digging at each other, I would have guessed you were either good friends or blood enemies. I have brothers, myself, so I

43

know that the line between the two can get a little blurry sometimes."

"How bad is it?" Clint asked, craning his neck so he could get a better look over the doctor's broad shoulders.

Getting up and walking over to a nearby table, Garza said, "The bullet took out a good piece beneath Peter's arm, but I don't think it caught anything too important. Most of the damage is close to the surface and since the bullet passed through completely, I'd say it could have been a lot worse."

"When will I be able to work again?" Peter asked.

"I'll need to stitch this up, but give it a couple days to heal and that should be plenty. It might be a little longer for you to do any delicate work, though."

Clint pulled up a chair and sat down next to Peter while the doctor began sewing shut the holes made by the passing bullet. "Anything I can do?"

"I could do with a spot of gin," Peter replied almost immediately.

Noticing the way the Englishman winced every time the doctor's needle pierced his flesh, Clint nodded and kept talking. It seemed to do a good job of taking his friend's mind off of things enough for Peter to be a bit more comfortable during the process. "Since you're not going anywhere, how about you tell me what all that was about back there."

Even though he was doing a good job of keeping a straight face as the needle bit into him, Peter was getting a tad pale. "This Major fellow has approached me before. On other contracts I've acquired. He's the typical sort of fellow who I would normally refuse to work for."

"Really?" Clint said. "How so?"

"You know the sort. Special orders to improve the speed of their draw. Extended range on rifles meant for hunting anything on two legs. A man in my trade can sniff out those kind fairly easily. There's a certain nastiness about them."

Clint nodded. "Yeah. I know what you mean."

"So do I," Doctor Garza said as he pulled his threat taut and tied it off.

"I don't know how he heard about this," Peter said. "But I doubt he'll let it pass just because we turned back the first blokes he sent at us."

"What else can you tell me about this man?"

Peter took a deep breath as some of the color flushed back into his face. "I can tell you a bit more, but I certainly hope you intend on getting that gin sometime soon. I could sure use it."

"All right then," Clint said as he stood up. "I guess I'll just be a good little colonist and fetch the Lord of the Manor his drink. I might also do a little scouting along the way."

Peter wasn't the only one smiling at that one. Even Doctor Garza laughed under his breath as he started in on stitching shut the hole where the bullet had left Peter's body.

"Anything for you, Doc?" Clint asked.

"Nothing from the saloon, thanks, but you might do me a favor and stop by the sheriff's office. It sounds to me like Peter here might need someone watching over him for a bit after upsetting this particular bunch of people."

"You read my mind." On his way out, Clint stopped in front of a small potbellied stove which was situated in the middle of the room. He held his hands, palms out, in front of the warm black steel and rubbed them together until some of the chill was gone. Stomping his feet managed to wake up his toes a bit and after that, he headed for the door.

There was something about the doctor that stuck in Clint's mind. It wasn't anything sinister, but more of a feeling that there was more to the Mexican than what he could see. For the moment, he didn't have any problem trusting the physician and that gut instinct was enough for Clint to leave Peter there for the time being.

One thing he didn't like, however, was the fact that both of the other men seemed to know more about this

Major person than they were telling him. Clint was un-
happy enough being put in the line of fire and he surely
didn't intend on taking it lying down.

Just as Clint was thinking that, he noticed the doctor
look up from what he was doing to fix him with an earnest
stare.

"Be careful," Garza said, as if he knew exactly what
was going through Clint's mind. "I don't want to be working on you anytime soon."

Clint nodded and said, "I appreciate the sentiment, Doc.
But if things do go from bad to worse, I think you might
want to worry about someone else besides me."

Confident that Peter was in good hands for the moment,
Clint waved to the older man and walked through the
door.

TWELVE

It was much too early in the day for the Double Diamond to be doing much by way of business. In fact, the only reason it stayed open at all during the morning was because there were a few hard-nosed card players who made it worth the owner's while to keep his doors open. Of course, it also didn't hurt that the owner himself often-times played games of poker that lasted well over three days.

Although he wasn't involved in such a game at the moment, the owner of the gambling club was sitting at a table and he was playing a hand of five card draw. Having just received the two cards he'd asked for, the burly, barrel-chested figure sitting behind a modest stack of chips took a look at his new hand and looked back up at the other players without showing the slightest hint of emotion upon his face.

"What'll it be, Major?" a portly young man in a dirty white shirt asked.

"Raise seventy-five," the man referred to as Major answered. He was dressed in a gray satin vest over a pearl-white shirt. His gray trousers were held up by silk suspenders which drew two straight lines over a mildly swollen belly. His face was wide and expressive, covered with

47

silvery hair that somehow crossed over from making him look old to simply distinguished.

The Major's face was covered mostly by a thick mustache that was waxed at both ends as well as a pair of thick sideburns which nearly touched the corners of his mouth. A large, bulbous nose jutted from his head and a pair of bushy eyebrows danced over it as he glanced from one face to another.

Just then, the front door to the club was thrown open and two men shuffled inside. One man was helping another even though his own steps weren't coming very easily. Apart from the men playing cards and one other working behind the bar, there wasn't anyone else inside the place so the new arrivals drew every bit of attention their way.

The Major was especially interested in the pair who'd just come through his door, but that interest didn't even register in his cold, glassy eyes. He tapped an impatient finger upon the table after a few more seconds had passed and finally started snapping his fingers.

"Are you gonna call or are we going to watch the stage show over there?" the Major asked.

It was the portly man's turn to put up or shut up and he was currently twisted around to look at the other men standing at the door. "Maybe we should see what those t—"

"It was a simple question. Are you gonna call or not?"

"Sure," the other man said, turning back around toward the game in progress. "I'll call."

Once that man's chips hit the middle of the table, it was the third player's turn to bid. Knowing better than to say what was on everyone else's mind, he glanced over to the Major and tossed in some chips. "Raise fifty."

By that time, the two men had spotted the Major and were making their way toward that table. "We ran into some trouble," one of the men said once he'd made it halfway across the room. It was the man who'd led the trio of intruders into Peter's shop only a few minutes ago.

His only remaining partner was helping him walk despite the gunshot wounds which hurt more with every passing second.

The Major's eyes flicked up toward the two men wearing bloodied clothes and then dropped back down to his cards. "See your fifty and raise another sixty."

"Major, we're hurt."

Wincing once he got a closer look at the other two, the bartender looked over to the card table. "That's no lie, Major. They're bleeding all over the floor."

That caught The Major's eye once again, but also sparked a trace of anger in his eyes. "That's why I specifically instructed them to meet me next door. Since they insist on interrupting my game rather than go to a doctor, they're just going to have to wait until this hand is over."

"See your fifty and raise twenty-five."

"Jesus Christ, can't you see my men are bleeding over there? You still want to keep raising? I'll see your twenty-five and raise another fifty."

"Major, Davey didn't make it and we're shot up here."

Without taking his eyes from the man seated next to him, the Major furrowed his brow and said, "A man's dead and two more are wounded and yet you still insist on keeping me here with this betting."

"You can fold whenever you want," the other gambler said.

"No I can't. I'm a sick man and not a master to my compulsions. You know that. I can't help but raise another fifty."

Obviously in the grip of his own compulsions, the portly man in the hot seat at the card table took a look at the pot in front of him and then glanced over his shoulder. The first thing he noticed was the blood that had soaked into the two men's clothes. Next, the smell of burnt gunpowder drifted over from them and reached his nose.

"Jesus, those two look bad."

"And they're waiting to see me," the Major said. "But I need to finish this first."

"You sure ain't right," the other gambler finally said. "I fold. Just go do whatever you need to before someone dies here in front of me."

Placing his cards facedown upon the table, the Major smirked and raked in his chips. "Feelings don't have any place at a poker table. You'd do well to remember that."

The smirk on the winner's face was more than simply victorious. It had a way of subtly mocking the other gambler for caving in his hand and giving up the chips. It said that the Major would have had no trouble letting those other two men bleed to death before he conceded the game.

"Cash these out," the Major said to the man working behind the bar. "Now, let's see what's got you two so riled up."

THIRTEEN

The Major was a big man and moved with slow, stomping steps. He wasn't impeded by his weight, but instead he moved slowly because he didn't like anyone telling him to go faster. He moved at his own pace and the rest of the world just had to get used to it. Even as the two wounded men shuffled behind him, the Major walked first through the front door and didn't hold it open for the others following in his wake.

He took a moment to fill his lungs with the crisp wintry air and then took his sweet time walking next door into the narrow building attached to the Double Diamond. This time, he did hold open the door but that was just so he could hurry the other two along.

Finally, after entering the smaller building and setting himself down onto a stool in a fairly empty room, the Major let out a breath and motioned for the others to take a seat.

Apart from that stool, the room had a small rolltop desk, a wobbly table, and half a dozen chairs. Normally, the front room of the building was never used and it had the thick layers of dust to prove it. Not making the other two men follow him all the way into the back room was the Major's only concession.

"I suppose you want a doctor?" the Major said.

The man who'd led the intruders nodded weakly. "Yeah I think I need one."

"I'm sure someone from the Diamond has sent for one. In the meantime, why don't you tell me how come the three of you couldn't impose yourselves on some old craftsman."

"There was someone else there," the other gunman said. "He might have been hired by the old man, since he was good with that gun of his."

"Peter is no slouch himself," the Major pointed out.

"I know. He's the one that killed Davey."

The only expression that registered upon the Major's face was a distinct raising of his eyebrows. "Is that so? I didn't think Peter had it in him to draw blood."

"Oh he did alright. They both did."

"And what about the package I sent you there to retrieve? Did you manage to get your hands on it?"

The youngest of the two gunmen looked over to the wounded leader. Another couple seconds drifted by before the older of the two shook his head.

Hearing that, the Major's face shifted to the unreadable granite that it had been while playing cards. "Did you even get a look at it?"

Another shake of the head.

"I see. Do you think you at least know where he keeps it?"

"There was a chest he reached for," the younger of the two gunmen offered. "But that might have just been where he kept the gun he used on us."

The Major didn't even acknowledge that comment with a glance. Instead, he reached into the pocket of his vest and pulled out a pouch of tobacco and a sheet of rolling paper. "So you didn't accomplish much, did you," he said while sprinkling tobacco onto the paper and twisting it into a cigarette. "What can you tell me about this other man besides the obvious fact that he was good with a firearm and smarter than all three of you combined?"

Wincing as pain stabbed through him, the older of the

two gunmen drew in a breath. His skin had gone from looking merely pale to taking on a dull, waxy look. "He told me to tell you that you weren't going to get what you were after and that Peter was his friend."

"That's something, at least. Unfortunately, it's nowhere near enough."

Both of the gunmen lowered their eyes and shifted in their seats like scolded schoolboys. The silence was heavy with the smell of blood and the intensity of the Major's stare as his eyes dug tunnels through the other two men.

Unable to keep to himself any longer, the man who'd acted as leader for the intruders clenched his jaw and spoke through his teeth. "When is that doctor coming?"

"Why? Is it starting to hurt?"

The wounded man tried to keep silent, but broke down after a second or two. "Yeah. It hurts."

"Good. You deserve to hurt for how badly you fucked this up." Clenching his cigarette between his lips, the Major stood up and walked past the two others on his way to the door. His hand dug under his vest where he kept his matches. "Maybe I should check on that doctor."

"I'd appreciate it."

The Major stopped and moved behind the other two chairs. His hand went past his matches and to the small of his back. "Then again," he said as he pulled a polished stiletto from the scabbard hidden beneath his vest, "maybe I should just cut my losses."

With that, the Major's hand flashed outward and placed the stiletto's nine-inch blade against the younger of the two men's throats. One quick motion was all it took to cut the man open from ear to ear. By the time the first labored gurgle could be heard, the already wounded man felt the bite of steel across his own neck. Warm blood poured down both men's shirts and their breath escaped through the neat slits beneath their chins.

He stepped back around so he could look down into the two men's faces as they flopped in their chairs and grabbed for their throats. That sight seemed to truly amuse him as he sheathed his stiletto and took a match from his pocket

After lighting his cigarette and flicking the spent match to the floor, the Major inhaled a lungful of smoke and blew it toward the dying men."Since you obviously don't have the sense God gave a mule, I'll tell you that the doctor isn't coming."

The two intruders died in the order they'd been cut. First the younger let out his final breath and then the older one stopped struggling against the inevitable. That one's eyes were open and lifeless when the Major flicked his ashes onto the corpse's pasty forehead.

FOURTEEN

Clint stopped the first man with a badge that he spotted on his way back to the gambling house where he'd fol lowed the two remaining intruders. It was a busy time of the morning right after most folks had eaten breakfast and before most of them would think about lunch. It was the time of day when shopping and other such errands were run and the streets were fairly bustling with people.

With the sun just breaking through the clouds, Clint's eye was drawn to a glint of light on steel which just happened to come from a nearby man's chest. Clint had been headed toward that man anyhow since the figure was strolling down the street and tipping his hat to all he met. He didn't seem to be shopping and didn't really seem to have a destination in mind.

It looked like that man was making rounds, which would mean he was a keeper of the peace. That might not have been flawless logic, but it panned out well enough this time around. The figure did turn out to be a deputy and he was more than happy to follow up on Clint's suggestion that he check in with Doctor Garza. From there, Clint knew the doctor would fill in the rest of the spaces and make sure Peter had someone protecting him while he got some much-deserved rest.

In the meantime, Clint figured whoever was moving

against Peter was taking a bit of a rest as well. That would
give Clint a good opportunity to get a look at this Major
and see what type of man he was dealing with. Anyone
that would kill to get their way couldn't be all that good.
And if this weapon was as impressive as Peter was making it sound, that made the situation all the more perilous.

Clint couldn't let a killer get their hands on that gun.
Even though he had yet to see the apple of Peter's eye,
he knew the Englishman's talents well enough to respect
his word.

After pointing the deputy in the right direction, Clint
made his way down the street and headed to the Double
Diamond Club, which was the last place he'd seen those
two men who'd threatened Peter. The first thing he tried
to do was open the door to the narrow building next to
the gambling club.

It was locked.

No big surprise there, but Clint had thought it was
worth a try. The next thing he tried was knocking on the
door. He got another surprise when the knock was answered in just a few seconds. There was the clunk of a
latch being pulled back followed by the door itself swinging inward. A man in his twenties with a face full of
whiskers peered through the crack and met Clint's gaze.

"Something I can do for you?" he asked.

Clint moved his head to the right so he could get a look
past the man at the door and into the room. He only got
a split second before the other man stepped closer to block
the opening completely, but that was just enough time to
get a glimpse past him.

From what Clint could see, the room just past the front
door was sparsely furnished. There was a fair amount of
activity going on in there and he could see at least two
figures hunched over and shuffling toward the back of the
room. It seemed as though those two were dragging something. Whatever it was, it required both arms for them to
carry it.

Mulling over the quick look he'd gotten, Clint shifted

his attention to the man who now filled up his entire field
of vision. It wasn't hard to tell that the greeter wasn't at
all happy to see him.

"Is the Major here?" Clint asked as casually as possible.

The other man seemed suspicious, but not overly so.
"He's at his club next door. What do you want with him?"

"I'd rather discuss that with the Major."

"Then do it. Just get the hell away from this door before
it gets slammed in your face."

Clint stepped back and made sure his hands and feet
were clear before the greeter followed through on his
promise. Sure enough, the door slammed shut hard enough
to rattle the floorboards and the heavy latch dropped into
place on the other side.

Clint hadn't been expecting a red carpet, but he'd managed to get enough information to make the trip worth his
while. Not only did he see those other two inside the place
dragging something heavy, but he'd managed to catch a
whiff of a familiar scent.

Death.

Not only did a man's heart stop when he died, but every
other part of him did as well. The bowels relaxed, which
gave death a particularly pungent stench, especially when
mixed with the coppery smell of blood that drifted
through that door as well.

Someone had been killed inside that narrow building.
Judging by what Clint had seen, he figured at least two
men had been killed in there and it had happened recently
enough that the bodies were just now being dragged away.

Just then, Clint got the sinking feeling that he was out
of luck if he'd been expecting to meet up with those two
gunmen ever again. That didn't make him too sad, but it
did show him that he was dealing with someone even
more bloodthirsty than he'd initially expected.

He thought about all of this as he stepped away from
the doorway and walked over to the neighboring Double
Diamond Club. A stiff wind tore down the street just as
he was opening the club's front door. The cold raked

through his entire body and sank all the way down to the marrow in his bones. It howled loudly as it rushed between the buildings, down the street and through anyone else that got in its way. Everyone else on the street clutched their coats and scarves closer to their bodies and stopped what they were doing until the wind passed.

But Clint couldn't afford to stop now, even for just a second. Strangely enough, that was how most of his life was. Whether it was his choice or not, Clint took most of his steps like he'd been swept up in a stampede. As dangerous as that was, he'd grown to like it over the years.

When he opened the door, the wind pushed him inside like an invisible hand, shoving him into the lion's den.

FIFTEEN

As far as lion's dens went, the Double Diamond Club was a pretty nice one. The building itself felt a little narrow, but that was just because it was so much deeper than it was wide. There was a bar along the left side which stretched back for half of the room. At the moment, there was only one person on either side of the bar: one was drinking and the other was pouring.

The rest of the place was filled with tables. That was the main difference that separated a gambling club from a saloon. Saloons had piano players, stages, and other forms of entertainment for its customers. Gambling clubs were designed with one purpose and that was to gamble. If something didn't further that goal, then it had no place inside one of those clubs.

Gambling clubs were built to host games and cater to the players, and the Double Diamond was no different. There were tables for poker, faro and blackjack. There was the bar to satisfy the gamblers' thirst and stairs leading to a second floor at the back of the room. Only two of the tables were occupied at the moment, so Clint started walking back toward the one with the most chairs filled.

He made it about three steps before he heard a vaguely familiar voice.

"Clint, over here!"

Turning to look in the direction of the voice, Clint tried not to look so annoyed for being picked out so soon after his entrance. It would have been nice, after all, if he could have gotten a little closer to his goal before being announced.

Whatever annoyance he might have felt immediately began to fade, however, once he got a look at who had called out his name. He almost didn't recognize the woman coming out from behind the bar at first. But it was hard to forget the smile on the woman's face, especially when it was framed by her flowing blonde hair.

Clint walked over to the bar and got there just as the blonde stepped around it. "Hello, Amanda."

"I didn't think I'd see you for a while, yet." Cocking her head and winking flirtatiously, she asked, "Couldn't keep away, huh?"

"I'll bet that look gets you a lot of tips from the high rollers," Clint said.

"Are you trying to tell me it's not working on you?"

"I was going to try to tell you that, but I doubt I could pull it off."

"Good," she said, stepping up close enough to reach out and brush her hand along his cheek. "I was thinking for a moment that I was losing my touch."

Even though Clint didn't say so with words, he knew damn well that she certainly wasn't losing her touch. Amanda was dressed in a dark red dress that hugged every one of her impressive curves. She had a tight, supple body that made him think she might have been a dancer. She'd even moved like a dancer when she'd come around the bar to greet Clint moments ago. Every move she made had a little bit of grace and by the look in her eyes she knew that without having to be told.

That innate confidence made her attractive as well. Nobody made arrogance attractive, but self-confidence was something else. Amanda spoke like a woman who was sure of herself and that would have impressed Clint coming from anyone. Coming from a woman as beautiful as

Amanda, it stirred something deep inside of him.

His senses on the lookout for anything that might have been a threat, Clint was still taking in what was going on in the rest of the room. As he spoke to Amanda, he could tell that other eyes were upon him. Namely, they were eyes belonging to a large figure sitting at the emptier of the two occupied card tables.

"Can I get you a drink?" Amanda asked. "And before you get the wrong idea, getting drinks is what I get paid to do, so don't make me look bad in front of my boss." When she said that last part, Amanda reflexively glanced toward the back of the room.

"Is your boss here?" Clint asked.

Leaning in a little closer, she placed one hand on the bar, arching her back and lifting one foot off the floor as though she was being swept off her feet. Even though the breathtaking view down the front of her dress was anything but accidental, Clint soaked it up all the same.

Amanda paused, took a deep breath, lowered her voice and said, "He's the dandy with the gray whiskers and suspenders."

"Is he the Major?"

"You've heard of him?" She laughed once, rolled her eyes and dropped back onto both feet. "That's silly. Obviously you must've heard of him. Do you know the Major?"

"Only by reputation." This time when Clint looked over to that card table in the back of the room, he didn't try to disguise what he was doing in the least. He turned to fix his eyes on the man with the silvery mustache and sideburns, only to find that the Major was glaring right back at him.

Although the older man's gaze seemed to drive completely through Clint's skull, it only lasted for a second before the Major turned his attention to a more attractive subject.

"He seems to like you," Clint said.

Amanda looked over to the Major's table and smiled

bright enough to light up the whole room. She stood on her tiptoes, not so much to look over anything, but to give the other man something he could look over for himself. When she waved at the Major, Amanda bounced just enough on her feet to set her curves into motion. The bounce was constricted by her tight-fitting dress, but most definitely made the impression she'd intended.

"He does like me," Amanda said just loud enough for Clint to hear. "But then again, can you blame him?"

"Not at all," Clint replied without hesitation.

SIXTEEN

"Maybe I can show you up to one of our rooms," Amanda said. "You are staying in town for the night, aren't you?"

"I am."

"And have you booked another room yet?"

Clint smiled and shook his head. "Good lord, you must pull in a lot of money for this place. I'll bet you could sell a room to someone who owns a hotel here in town."

"Well, I still have a little while before anyone'll need me down here, so I thought I could show you around. If you'd rather me leave you alone, then I could do that too."

Watching her as she went through her act, Clint couldn't help but be charmed by the blonde. She was more playful than manipulative, but it all wound up the same way. That old saying about catching more bees with honey must have been true after all.

His first impulse had been to take the blonde up on her offer. It didn't matter if she was trying to hustle a commission for the room or not. She was the kind of woman a man wanted to be with. Even so, Clint had been around enough women to be able to read them a little better than that. There had been something in Amanda's eyes from the moment Clint had looked into them. Just so long as he was more aware than the average drunk gambler, Clint was confident he could tell if he was being hustled too badly.

But Clint hadn't gone into the Double Diamond Club to check in on Amanda. He'd gone there to meet up with the man playing cards in the back of the room. He needed to have a word with this Major and see if he could find out something about him. Clint had every intention of making the other man pay for what he'd tried to do, but it was never smart to go up against someone blindly.

Since time was of the essence, Clint was hoping to get as much out of the Major as he could in as little time as possible. To do that, he needed to make the Major lower his defenses. The quickest path through a man's defenses was by getting under his skin. And the more Clint stood there, the more certain he was that he'd found a way to do just that.

"All right, you can spare me the pouty lip," Clint said to the blonde. As he spoke, Clint moved in just close enough to encourage Amanda's playful affections. He reached up and brushed the tip of his finger along her soft bottom lip.

Amanda's smile broadened and she moistened the part of her lip that Clint had touched with the pink tip of her tongue. "Maybe I should watch my step around you, Clint. You seem like you might enjoy getting me up in one of these rooms."

"I didn't even know this place rented rooms until you mentioned it. And no, I wouldn't mind having you in one with me at all."

"We only rent to players, so you'll have to sit in on a few games to make sure I don't get in trouble."

"This is working out to be more expensive by the minute."

"Don't worry. The only thing you'll have to pay for is the gambling. If you gamble enough, I can usually convince the Major to let the room go without charge. Then again, you might not make it down to do much card playing for a while."

At the other end of the room, the Major was seething. He wasn't doing anything to betray his emotions, but Clint could feel the tension coming from the other man like heat radiating off a rock that had baked on the floor of a desert.

He stoked those fires just a little bit by giving the Major a smug grin before turning back toward Amanda and kissing her lightly on the lips. "I hope I'm not being too forward," Clint said to her.

"If you didn't do that soon, I was about to think you were beyond my reach."

"I seriously doubt any man with a pulse is beyond your reach." With the jealous glare of the Major burned into his mind, Clint knew his last statement was as true as words could be.

Clint offered Amanda his arm and she immediately hooked hers around it. As she led him toward the stairs in the back of the room, Amanda walked with a swing in her step that allowed her hip to glide against Clint's. He was close enough to smell the subtle amount of perfume she wore, which caused his heart to beat just a little bit faster.

As they passed the card table, Clint noticed that the Major was following their every move with his cold, expressionless eyes. The older man continued playing as he tracked them, but there was no mistaking the fact that he wasn't at all happy with Clint's choice of company.

There wasn't a doubt in Clint's mind that the Major was feeling something burrowing deep beneath his skin.

SEVENTEEN

Upstairs, the Double Diamond Club had a row of rooms which apparently were offered to their loyal players. Clint wasn't surprised at all to find them there since most gambling clubs liked to keep their spenders as close to the tables as possible at all times. More than likely, if there wasn't a kitchen downstairs, there were runners who would bring meals to the tables rather than have any gamblers leave.

What did surprise Clint about the upstairs was how well decorated it was. Normally, rooms found in such places were the bare minimum since those who stayed in them really didn't spend too much time there. Clint had slept in his fair share of gambling houses. The beds were always comfortable, but not too much so. The rooms were a place to pass out for a few hours. Nothing more.

So far, the hallway over the Double Diamond was fancier than all other gambling houses' rooms combined. There was a rug on the floor that ran the entire length of the hall and there were enough lanterns along the walls to make the place downright cheery once the sun went down.

Amanda led him to a room in the middle of the hall. The door was marked with a number 3 painted in black at eye level. She opened the door and stepped inside, closing the door once Clint was in there with her.

"Here you go," she said, walking toward a large bed and running her hand along the thick cotton comforter. "Not bad for a poker hall, huh?"

Clint took a quick look around and noticed there was a chair against one wall and a small dresser with a wash basin on top of it. A row of small square windows lined the opposite wall and were just low enough for Clint to look through. They were high enough, however, to make it awkward to stand at them for too long.

It wouldn't do to have a player wasting time looking at the street when there were plenty of chairs downstairs that needed to be filled.

But Clint wasn't concerned with the windows. He wasn't concerned with the sturdy, comfortable chairs or even the dresser which appeared to be a fairly expensive piece. Instead, he couldn't get his mind off of Amanda who'd walked around the bed and was leaning with her back against the wall next to the headboard.

One hand was positioned over her midsection and the other drifted down so she could touch the pillow with her fingertips. She reminded Clint of an old painting. The light from the little windows formed bright beams which touched her hair and made the strands sparkle like gold.

"You're so quiet," she said. "What's the matter?"

"Would it be too dramatic if I said that you took my breath away?"

Amanda smiled and lowered her eyes. When she looked up again, she was still smiling, but in a relaxed, comfortable way. "That is a bit much, but I don't mind hearing it. Not from you."

"Good," Clint said as he moved forward. "Because that's how I'm feeling right about now." He lifted his arms and pressed his hands against the wall on either side of Amanda's shoulders.

When he bent his elbows, he brought himself in close enough that he could feel the heat from her body against his own. From where he was, Clint could tell that what little perfume she wore was in her hair. Amanda's skin had a sweetness of its own, but it was nothing that could have been put into a bottle.

. Clint took his time savoring the way her heat and scent moved around him. With a couple deep breaths, he felt those parts of her enter inside him. He could hear her breathing as well. The longer he went without talking and the closer he got to her, the quicker her breaths became. Finally, he felt her hands moving on his body. Her fingers drifted along Clint's stomach and then slowly moved up over his chest.

"I knew you were trouble," she whispered while gently kissing Clint's neck. She worked her way up until her teeth closed around his earlobe and began gently nibbling. "Ever since I first laid eyes on you, I knew you were trouble."

"Is that so?" Clint's hands were off the wall and roaming freely over Amanda's body by now. Her figure was lean and muscular and yet she still felt soft and yielding beneath his touch. "If I'm the one that's supposed to be trouble," Clint said, "then how come it was you that lured me up to this room?"

Amanda pressed both palms flat against Clint's chest and pushed him back as she took a step forward. "I brought you up here so I could do this," she said as she pushed him onto the mattress. "And something tells me that you can get away from here any time you want. The only thing is, I couldn't think of one reason why you'd want to."

As she spoke, Amanda worked Clint's gun belt open and then started in on his pants. She got both off of him in no time at all and was soon pulling open his shirt. She smiled seductively and let out a low moan when she felt him reach up and start caressing her breasts through the fabric of her dress.

Even with her clothes still on, Clint could feel Amanda's erect nipples as he massaged her soft curves. After watching her move and feeling her next to him for the last several minutes, Clint had been unable to think about much else besides getting his hands on her. Now that he could indulge those desires, he let his hands go wherever they wanted. She didn't seem to mind at all.

Straightening her back so she could look down at him, Amanda moved her hands up along her own body, sliding over Clint's as she moved over her breasts. She was straddling him with her knees on either side of his hips and when she rose up over him, Amanda ground her hips back and forth over Clint's erection.

Her eyes never left his as she reached down to gather up her skirt and pull it up around her waist, revealing the lace undies underneath. Holding back the skirt with one hand behind her body, she reached down with the other and began slowly stroking Clint's penis. Amanda moved her hips forward so she could rub his hard shaft between her legs, giving him a sample of the damp heat that waited for him there.

Something in the back of Clint's mind told him that he could be making a big mistake. By the look on the Major's face, if the older man decided to pay him a visit just then, there would be hell to pay.

But then Clint felt the contour of Amanda's pussy through the lace which now clung to her skin. She was rubbing him against herself and starting to moan with pleasure.

It might have been an awfully big gamble, but Clint figured he was in just the place for it.

EIGHTEEN

For the moment, Clint allowed himself to push aside everything else in his mind except for Amanda and the feel of her body against his own. The rest of the world was gladly put aside when he pulled aside the thin material of her panties and let her guide his penis into her.

Amanda's touch was firm yet gentle as she gripped his shaft and lifted herself just enough to get over him. She let out a long, satisfied sigh as she lowered herself down again, savoring the feel of his hard flesh driving deeply between her thighs. Allowing her skirt to flow behind her, Amanda started to move back and forth as she ground her hips against Clint's. Her muscles strained and flexed beneath her skin as she rode him with building intensity.

Clint looked up at her and placed his hands upon her hips, guiding her motions just enough to give them both the most pleasure. He watched as she slid her hands up along her sides and then through her hair. As she let her blonde strands pass through her grasp, she arched her back and lifted herself up on top of him. From there, not only did she rock back and forth, but she began bouncing up and down as well. Amanda clenched her thighs tightly around him as she rode his cock, her breathy moans becoming louder with every second.

Clint pushed his head back against the mattress as a

wave of pleasure surged through him. When he looked up
again, Amanda was falling toward him, her upper body
lowering until she had to brace herself with her hands on
either side of his head.

The instant she was close enough to him, Clint used
both hands to start pulling the clothes from her body. With
her continuing to ride him, it was hard for Clint not to
give in completely and tear the material apart with his
bare hands. He did send a few buttons flying through the
air, however, but the dress itself remained in one piece.

As the garment came up and over her head, Amanda
shook her hair free so that it flowed down over both of
her shoulders. She stopped moving for a second and
wrapped her arms around herself, covering her breasts and
upper torso. Her eyes drifted down until she was looking
at the strip of lace still bunched around her waist

Without missing a beat, Clint picked her up off of him,
rolled onto his side and then dropped her down so her
back hit the mattress. Positioning himself between her
legs, he reached down and tore the panties off of her with
a single motion. Amanda let out a surprised yelp as she
felt her last bit of clothing ripped completely off her body.

The surprised look was still on her face as Clint moved
his cock between the moist lips between her legs and
pushed inside of her once again. As he buried himself as
deep as he could go, he kept his eyes locked on her face,
watching the way her expression changed bit by bit.

First her eyes were wide and her mouth was open as if
she was about to let out a long moan. No sound came
from her lips, however, except for a sigh which came from
the back of her throat. As he slid further into her, Clint
saw her eyes start to close and her head begin to tilt back
against the bed. Amanda's mouth stayed open and the
corners curled into a satisfied grin.

She finally let out the moan she'd been holding back
once Clint's hips met hers and he was all the way inside.
With her eyes clenched shut, she wrapped her arms

around him and pushed her hips forward as though she
wanted to feel just how deep he could go.

Clint slid one hand beneath her head and moved the
other down along her body, stopping once he felt the tight
curve of her buttocks in his grasp. He moved slowly in
and out of her, picking up speed when he felt Amanda's
fingertips dig a little more into his back.

Their breathing was picking up speed at the same rate
and their bodies slowly wriggled together as Clint thrust
between her open legs. At one point, he lifted her backside
off the bed and pumped into her hard. That caused
Amanda to suck a breath in and let it out in a throaty cry.

Now that she'd started to get louder, Amanda lost herself in the heat of the moment and cried out every time
Clint pounded into her. One of her legs was halfway en-
twined with his and she let Clint's hands move her any
way they saw fit.

Although he could feel that he had complete control of
her, Clint also felt that she was still guiding him now and
then. Every so often, she would lift her hips or pull him
in closer, not letting him go until he rubbed against the
precise spot that would make her scream just a little
louder than the last time.

With her chest pressed tightly against his own, Clint
could feel Amanda's heart pounding like a drum inside
of her. The muscles in her body became taut and as her
climax approached, Clint could even feel her contracting
around his penis, massaging him in a way that pushed
him quickly over his own personal edge.

They came together, their bodies sweating and their
hands moving freely over the other's naked skin. Even as
his own climax was subsiding, Clint thrust once more between her legs, causing Amanda's eyes to snap open and
her body to tense one more time.

NINETEEN

"Oh my god," she said when she was once again able to for a complete sentence. "You are full of surprises."

Clint looked down at her and focused on the warmth of her body against his own. Stroking a few strands of golden hair away from her face, he said, "You can't tell me this came a surprise. I feel like I fell into one of your traps."

"I'm offended, Clint. You should know better than to call a woman out like that." Pretending to work herself into a huff, Amanda rolled onto her stomach and crossed her arms beneath her head.

Clint couldn't help but take a moment to let his eyes wander down the alluring curve of her spine and linger on her tight, rounded backside. "If you're trying to punish me right now, you're doing a lousy job."

She glanced over at him with a bit of fire in her eyes, but was unable to keep up the angry charade any longer. Swatting his knee, she curled her legs back and kicked the air in a way that only made her look all the more enticing.

"You're not only trouble, but you've got a smart mouth, too," she said.

"It takes a smart ass to know one," Clint shot back.

74   J. R. ROBERTS

Before she could say anything else, he reached out and started to tickle her ribs and back.

Amanda ignored it at first, but was soon laughing into the mattress and squirming halfheartedly to get away.

"Oh no you don't," Clint said as he moved in closer and tightened his grip. "You're not going anywhere."

He was laying on his side and she'd managed to roll onto her side facing away from him. Rather than make a real effort to escape his teasing, she wriggled against him in a way similar to the way she'd brushed against him on their way up to the room. This time, however, there were no clothes between them and her soft, trim body was grinding directly against his.

"I'm not going anywhere?" she said in a challenging tone. "And just what are you gonna do about it?"

Clint wrapped his arms around her so that he could brush against the sides of Amanda's breasts. "I might hold you here and not let go. Or," he said as his thumbs moved out to feel her erect nipples, "I might just make it so you don't want to leave."

Amanda was still moving, but now she'd started shifting her hips back and forth, grinding slowly against his stiffening cock. "Mmm, I like the sound of that second one," she purred. Reaching one hand back to slide through Clint's hair, she drew in a sharp breath as Clint's erection moved between her legs.

Her skin tasted sweet and a little salty as Clint started kissing her on the back of the neck, nibbling gently at the top of her spine beneath her thick golden hair. He was hard again and wanted to be inside of her with every ounce of his being.

As if reacting to that urgent desire, Amanda lifted her top leg and hooked it back so that it was resting on Clint's hip. From there, Clint could feel his shaft gliding over the warm moist spot between her thighs. His cock slipped between the delicate lips there and brushed against her clit as he pushed forward.

Amanda was turning to look back, but was unable to

kiss Clint on the mouth. That seemed to make her frustrated and anxious at the same time. Once again, she was breathing heavily and she reached out with both hands to touch Clint wherever she could. One hand dug through his hair and rubbed his neck, while the other massaged his inner thigh.

Finally, after feeling his rigid penis move over her pussy one more time, Amanda reached down and guided him inside of her. She moaned loudly as he entered her from behind. His shaft rubbed inside of her against spots he could only reach from that angle, sending her straight to the pinnacle of arousal in a matter of seconds.

Clint reached around to cup her breasts as he pumped in and out of her. Keeping one hand over her nipple, he used the other to reach down and rub small circles over her clit. She put her hand on top of his, feeling him pleasure her while letting his cock slide between her fingers.

It wasn't long before Amanda was arching her back against him as another scream caught in her throat. She didn't make a sound as yet another climax rippled through her body. Instead, every muscle tensed and her eyes were clenched shut so tightly that spots formed beneath her lids.

Clint felt a more intense orgasm as well. The combination of being inside of her as well as feeling her hands on his shaft made him pound into her even harder. Amanda's body felt hot now and perfectly conformed to his own as he moved in and out of her.

One more thrust and he exploded inside of her. Amanda's fragrant hair covered his face as he felt every inch of her back sliding against every inch of his front. He almost didn't have enough energy to move back as his climax subsided. When he did, he instantly regretted it since he could no longer feel her soft curves held tightly against him. She must have felt the same thing since Amanda rolled over and rested her head on Clint's chest. Her arm fell across him and she let out an exhausted breath.

"Now that truly was a surprise," she gasped.

"So my plan to keep you here worked?"

Amanda looked up at him and laughed. "I couldn't leave this bed right now even if I wanted to. I just hope I didn't make enough noise to distract the card games downstairs."

At that moment, Clint thought about what she'd just said and then pictured the card games that had been going on as he'd followed Amanda upstairs. One game in particular sprung to mind and Clint couldn't help but feel a mischievous smirk drift onto his face.

In fact, Clint could damn near picture the look on the Major's face if he did manage to hear Amanda crying out in the fit of passion from just above his head. If the older man wanted her as badly as it appeared when he'd glared at Amanda on Clint's arm, then he would be fit to be tied when his worst suspicions were proven true.

Although Clint had wanted to get under the Major's skin, it hadn't been his intention to bed down Amanda just for that purpose. She'd called the shots there on her own and Clint wasn't exactly the type of man to refuse a beautiful woman. The way it turned out might work in Clint's favor in more than the most obvious way.

Then again, getting too far under someone's skin might just push them to do things they might not have had the guts to do under normal circumstances. When he thought along those lines, Clint wondered if he should be ready for the door to his room to be kicked down at any moment by an angry man with gray hair and suspenders.

Amanda's fingertips were gliding over his chest, tracing gentle patterns through his hair. Her breasts were pressed against his shoulder and one leg was draped over his thighs. For a moment, Clint thought she might have fallen asleep. Then, she took a deep breath and looked up at him.

"What's that little smirk on your face?" she asked while nuzzling in a little closer.

"What smirk?"

"The one that makes you look like that old saying about

the cat that swallowed the canary. Are you feeling pretty good about yourself just because I dragged you up here and had my way with you?"

"Of course I am," Clint answered, his hand moving along her side and brushing the side of her breast. "But I was actually thinking that I feel more like another old saying."

"Which one's that?"

"The one about being careful what you wish for."

TWENTY

Clint took his time getting dressed, but also made sure that he didn't fall asleep. Not only did he not want to make Amanda uncomfortable by hurrying or seeming too anxious to get the Colt strapped around his waist, but he also wanted to put his own mind at ease. Whether it was during a fight or days before one, it was never a good idea to get too worked up about anything.

There had already been trouble and Clint knew that more was on its way. The best thing he could do in the meantime was to look into what had caused it and keep himself prepared for the inevitable. The Major would be waiting for him. In fact, Clint was counting on that.

The Major wasn't through with Peter either. That was another fact that Clint could take to the bank. But there was a lot that could go on between where he was and where things were headed. Clint knew that for certain, while arrogant men figured the deck was already stacked in their favor.

Keeping all of this in mind, Clint buckled his gun belt around his waist and reached for his hat. It had been sitting on the small table partially hanging over the water basin the last time he'd seen it. When it wasn't there this time, Clint spun around and looked toward the bed.

His eyes made it as far as the bed before they stopped.

Actually, it would have been more appropriate to say that they were stopped by the sight of Amanda kneeling on the bed facing him. She was completely naked except for Clint's hat, which she held over her pert breasts.

"Looking for this?" she asked with her familiar grin.

Clint moved forward and took the hat from her. She held onto it long enough so that she was pulled close to him until she fell forward into his arms. Dropping the hat onto his head, Clint wrapped his arms around Amanda, moving his hands over the smooth skin of her back.

"Thanks for keeping that warm for me," he said.

"Just returning the favor. You've kept me warmer than I've felt in a long time. Why do you have to get going so soon?"

"Don't you have a job to get to?"

She shrugged and dropped back onto the bed, sprawling out lazily in a way that almost made Clint think twice about leaving the room at all. "I'm already late for that, but I can get there in a minute. Besides, the Major is too sweet on me to fire me."

"That's what I'm worried about."

"Oh Clint, don't act all timid. You're not as good at it as I am."

"I'm serious. Do you think he's got it in him to hurt someone who crossed his path?"

"If someone crossed him, sure. But I work for the man. I'm not married to him." Laying there in front of him, Amanda seemed completely unconcerned with her nakedness. She made no attempt to cover herself and even let her hands wander lazily over herself.

Clint hadn't been planning on using his intimacy with her to his favor, but as long as the subject had already been broached, he didn't see any harm in following through. "What do you know about him, Amanda?"

"Who? The Major?"

"Yeah."

"I know he's rich and he owns this club."

"What else can you tell me?"

She took a breath and tapped her finger against her chin. "He's got a few men working for him. Rough types, if you know what I mean."

"Yeah. I think I know what you mean. How many of those rough types are there?"

"Hmm, maybe seven or eight."

"What do you think he would want with men like that?"

"Well, if you ask me, the Major can't have as much money as he does without some other business on the side. The Double Diamond is a successful place, but not that successful."

"Could this other business be illegal?" Clint asked.

Amanda shrugged, obviously losing interest in the conversation. "Could be. Isn't that why most people have hired guns working for them? Whatever else he may be into, I know he runs it out of the little building next door. I also know he cheats at cards," she said with a little wrinkle of her nose. "I caught him palming a king one time, but didn't say anything."

Shaking his head, Clint couldn't get over the way Amanda managed to keep her smile so innocent even when she was doing the least innocent things. "You're saving that one for a rainy day, huh?"

Amanda nodded. "Yep. And I might just cash it in if I wait around here much longer."

"Hey, I was the one trying to keep you from losing your job. You decided to wait around here without even reaching for your dress."

Her eyes drifted over to the dress and panties laying on the floor. Reaching down, she picked up the shredded underwear and let the lacy material dangle from her finger. "I don't have enough time to get another pair, so I guess I'll just have to go without for the rest of the night. Nobody should know, though. Nobody except you, that is."

Once again, Clint damn near jumped out of his clothes so he could join Amanda back on the bed. It took a will stronger than he thought possible to convince him to keep from doing otherwise.

"You're a devious woman, Amanda. Don't you dare think I'm through with you yet."

"You're still leaving?"

"I've got important matters to tend to." He kissed her once more and headed for the door. Picking up the key to the room and dropping it in his pocket, he said, "And don't make me come looking for you later tonight."

"Dream on, Adams," she said, feigning disinterest. "This train has left the station."

Clint stepped into the hall and shut the door. Before it closed, he caught one quick glance at Amanda's little grin. She was waving to him, knowing full well that he'd be watching her.

TWENTY-ONE

Just because he hadn't actually had sex with Amanda just to get to the Major, that didn't mean that Clint couldn't play up his walk down the stairs just a bit for the other man's benefit. As he descended back down to the main floor of the Double Diamond, Clint strutted like he was about to be sworn in as royalty. Part of him felt a little rotten for using his time with the blonde for another purpose, but he knew that the Major would draw his own conclusions no matter what had happened.

There was no harm in making sure that those conclusions at least served a greater purpose.

Any misgivings Clint might have had flew out the window once he got a look at what was waiting for him downstairs. For one thing, the club had filled up a little bit in the time he'd been in his room. It was only around noon, but already there were four more card games going on. A few more people were standing at the bar and their conversations filled the room with a low, continuous murmur.

What Clint was most concerned with was one game in particular. And more importantly, he wanted to focus in on one man playing at that particular game. Without making it seem obvious, Clint looked over to the table he'd been waiting to see. The Major was right where Clint had left him, still sitting with cards in his hand and chips stacked in front of him.

The older man made no effort to hide the fact that he was watching Clint come down those stairs. In fact, when he knew that Clint was looking directly at him, the Major turned so he could glare back at him directly, his eyes drilling straight into Clint's like thin daggers protruding from his skull.

Clint waited until he'd come down all the stairs before acknowledging the Major's stare. He did so with a tip of his hat and a friendly smile. That amiable combination only put more heat in the Major's eyes. The hatred flared up inside the older man to such a degree that Clint thought he might see steam rise up from his forehead.

If he'd wanted to get under the Major's skin, Clint knew at that moment that he'd done a hell of a job.

Without breaking his stride, Clint turned and headed for the bar. There were more empty spots toward the back of the room, so he sidled up to the polished oak structure and propped one foot upon the brass rail that ran the length of the bar just above the floor. Before he could lift his hand to summon the barkeep, Clint saw the man rush over to him.

"Good service here," Clint said as the barkeep came to a stop directly in front of him.

The barkeep was dressed in a wrinkled blue shirt with sleeves that were buttoned tightly over his wrists. A white apron spattered with various dark spots was tied around his waist. Appearing to be in his late thirties, the barkeep had skin as white as his apron and was nearly as skinny as the rail beneath Clint's foot.

"Major Waterman says I'm to get you whatever you'd like," the bartender said. "On the house."

Clint raised his eyebrows in a show of surprise. "On the house? Is this a courtesy because I'm renting a room here?"

"I don't know that for sure. All I know is I'm to pour you a drink."

"I'll take a beer, but only if you join me."

The barkeep looked confused as he reached beneath the countertop to produce a large mug. Glancing over to the Major's table, he glanced quickly back to Clint and then took out a shot glass. He then filled the mug with beer from a nearby tap and poured some whiskey into the shot glass.

"What's your name?" Clint asked.

"Uh . . . Marvin."

"Here's to you, Marvin." With that, Clint tipped back the mug and took a long sip of the foamy brew.

Marvin looked as though he didn't quite know what to make of the situation, but downed his whiskey anyway and immediately cleaned the shot glass with a rag that had been hanging from his apron string. "You're not a friend of Major Waterman are you?"

"Actually, I didn't even know he had a real name until you just said it. I'm new in town. The name's Clint Adams."

Marvin was slightly amused by Clint's humor, but not enough that he allowed it to show. His eyes kept darting from Clint to the table at the back of the room and his nervousness was still hanging around him like a fog. "Pleased to meet you, Clint. There's something else I was supposed to tell you."

"Let me guess. I'm supposed to get the hell out of town before the Major sends his men after me."

This time, Marvin couldn't help but laugh. It sounded more like an exaggerated cough and popped his shoulders up once toward his ears. "No, no. Major Waterman told me to steer you toward his table in the back."

"Is there a game going on?"

"There's always a game going on. If the Major is away from that chair for more than half an hour, he's either asleep or eating. I hope you brought some cash, though. I couldn't even to afford to sit in on his penny-ante games."

"I can hold my own, but tell me something." Clint

paused and leaned in just a bit. The gesture made the barkeep lean in as well and Clint lowered his voice even though there wasn't much of anyone else in the immediate vicinity. "I hear the Major can be a sore loser. Is that something I should look out for?"

Marvin obviously wasn't too comfortable talking on that subject. He stepped back and started nervously cleaning the top of the bar. "You'll have to look after yourself on that regard. I don't want any part of that kind of thing."

"Fair enough," Clint said as he took another sip of his beer and turned to walk toward the Major's table.

Even though Marvin hadn't been a fountain of information, the barkeep had told Clint plenty besides the Major's last name. Not only was there something underhanded about the game, but it was enough to make the barkeep genuinely fearful when talking about it. That was just as good as a straightforward warning in Clint's book.

Armed with the bits of information he'd gathered, Clint decided it was time to stop circling the target. He cleared his head of what had come before and stepped up to meet the Major.

TWENTY-TWO

Clint had to admit that he was impressed with the Major.

After toughing it through all the cold looks and hard stares he'd gotten from the other man, Clint had been half-expecting to be thrown into a fight the moment he got within swinging distance of that card table. But as soon as it was apparent that he was headed for the seat the Major had been saving for him, the older man leaned back in his chair and waited patiently for the new arrival.

Of course, it was still obvious to Clint that the man with the bushy mustache and barrel chest still wanted his blood more than anything at the moment. The tension was still brewing inside of Major Waterman and it wasn't the kind of thing to be hidden by a casual smile.

It was the Major's restraint that impressed Clint the most. Especially since he'd done his best to see if he could make the other man crack.

Clint made his way across the room and stood behind the empty seat at the Major's table. Major Waterman was sitting with both elbows propped on top of the table, shuffling a deck of cards. There were two others sitting at the table. One of them was a portly gentleman Clint recognized as the same man who'd been sitting there when he'd passed by with Amanda on his arm. The other was a younger man with a set of three scars marring his left cheek.

"I don't mean to interrupt your game, gentlemen," Clint said, "but I was told that you wouldn't mind if I sat in for a hand or two."

"You were told correctly," the Major said while getting to his feet. He extended his hand and fixed Clint with a powerful stare. "I'm Major Scott Waterman. United States Army, retired." Looking at each of the other two men, he pointed to each one in turn. "That's Marland," he said, indicating the portly man who'd been warming that seat for a good while. Turning his finger toward the younger man with the scars on his face, the Major said, "And that's Bill."

"Good to meet you all, I'm—"

"Clint Adams," Marland interrupted. "We know."

"Should I be honored that you all know me so well?" Clint asked. "Or should I be worried?"

Major Waterman lowered himself back down into his chair and began shuffling his card once again. "That all depends on why you're here."

"I'm just here to visit an old friend of mine," Clint said, lowering his eyes so he could take a good, hard look at the Major. "Peter Banks. You know him?"

Major Waterman hadn't spent so much time sitting at a poker table for nothing. His face betrayed not a single hint as to what he might truly be thinking and he even managed to pull off a moment or two where he looked as though he was really mulling over the question. Finally, his face brightened and he began to nod. "He's the gunsmith, right?"

"That's right."

"I've heard of him, but he doesn't frequent my club. Since I'm not the sort of man who requires his services, I'm afraid to say that I really don't know too much more about him."

"Well he knows you."

"Most people around here do, Mister Adams. It's all a

part of running a business such as this. A man has to
maintain a high profile and be something of a figurehead
if he wants to attract customers. Without such things, this
is just another house with card tables under its roof."

"That's true enough," Clint said. "But I've recently had
a run-in over at Peter's shop. Perhaps word might have
gotten back here about that."

The younger man with the scars had been tapping the
edge of the table impatiently with one of his betting chips.
He fidgeted in his chair like he was about to jump out of
his skin. Just then, he leaned forward and jumped through
the first opening he could find within the conversation.

"I heard there was some kind of fight over in that
shop," Bill said. "Gunshots and everything."

Looking over to the younger man, Clint only had to
study Bill's face for a second before he had all he needed.
Fortunately, the scars weren't nearly enough to cover up
the fact that Bill was hiding something. "Yeah, it was a
mess alright. Two men even wound up dead."

"I heard it was only one," Bill answered.

"Ugly rumors," Major Waterman said in a quick, biting
voice. The look in his eyes, on the other hand, was telling
Bill to shut the hell up before some harm came to him.
"All anyone knows is what they heard. Mister Adams was
there. He should know what went on better than all of
us."

"Actually," Clint said with a shrug, "it might have only
been one. One of those men took a pretty bad wound, so
I figured he must have crawled away somewhere to die
with his tail between his legs." As he spoke, his eyes
wandered over the faces of all three men around the table.
Even though he glanced toward each of them, Clint was
mainly studying Bill.

Sure enough, the younger man twitched when he heard
Clint's comment spoken in that disparaging manner. He
wanted to fire back with something, but managed to hold
his tongue. The effort was so easy to see that he might as
well have just come out with it.

Now that he knew for sure that Bill was one of the Major's gunmen, Clint figured it was safe to assume that Marland was working for him as well. That way, if he was wrong about the portly card player, it was an error on the side of caution rather than ignorance.

"Well, that's enough unpleasant talk," Clint said since he was finished with the subject anyway. "I came here to play some cards, so how about we get started?"

The Major allowed his stony facade to crack for just a moment as a smile curled his lip. "That's what I like to hear, Mister Adams. I've heard plenty of talk about you from plenty of others who've passed through my doors."

"Nothing too bad, I hope."

"Not at all. In fact, some of the sources were quite impressive. Why, I can remember Doc Holliday mentioning you by name a few years ago and he said you nearly cleaned him out at a game in Colorado."

Clint leaned back and waved away the comment as the Major began to deal out the first hand. "Doc talked a lot and he drank even more. I wouldn't worry about anything he said."

Flipping the cards out one by one, Major Waterman built up neat piles in front of each occupied seat. "Doc may have drunk a lot, but he was not the type of man to lie. Too bad about the way he died, in that sanitarium, and all."

Clint hadn't thought about the sickly gunfighter for some time. Holliday might not have been his favorite person in the world, but there were plenty worse out there.

"Yep," the Major went on, "that's too bad. Doc was a character and good for business. He had nothing but good things to say about you. I thought you might have been old friends."

"Like I said before, Doc was probably just talking, that's all."

"Don't sell yourself short. And speaking of which, I've sat in on a few games with Luke Short some time ago where your name came up as well."

Clint could tell he was the one being studied just then. The Major didn't give away anything in his eyes or any other way for that matter. Instead, Clint could just feel the other man's scrutiny like a shiver running through his spine.

Glancing around to Bill and Marland, Waterman said, "I'd watch myself if I were you, gentlemen. We might be in for a hell of a game."

TWENTY-THREE

Clint was fairly certain that he could trust much of the information he'd gotten so far. By that same token, he didn't for one moment think he could trust all of what he'd been told. Gathering good information was equal parts interrogation, instinct, and observation.

He knew that there would be more trouble headed in Peter's direction, but not right away. He also thought he could rely on the tip he'd been given that the Major had about eight men working for him. One was dead and another injured, which left six. Knowing for certain that at least one of those men was sitting at the card table with him with at least another one standing somewhere nearby, that left at least four more.

Another thing Clint could count on as gospel was that those remaining gunmen wouldn't make a move until they got the word from their boss. No matter how good a card player Major Waterman was, he hadn't done anything that struck Clint as a signal to any of those other men around him.

Although Clint oftentimes bet his life upon his instincts, he wasn't about to make Peter take that same wager. Time was short and, signal or not, Clint wanted to check up on the Englishman sooner rather than later. For the moment, he was in the middle of a card game and it was very easy to see that the Major was very much in his element.

Out of the three hands that had been dealt, the Major had won two. The third had gone to Marland, but the pot had been under twenty dollars. So far, Clint couldn't say if there was any cheating going on or not. He'd gotten a pair of fives the first hand, nothing for the second, and a low straight on the third.

He hadn't expected to win until he'd drawn a five to round out his straight only moments ago. Marland had beaten him, but only with a flush. Despite the fact that he'd lost a hand, Clint uncovered a definite clue in the way Marland let out a heavy breath after looking at the two cards that had been dealt to him to replace the ones he'd thrown away.

That breath struck Clint as a possible mannerism specific to the portly man when he got a good hand. Breathing patterns and motions of the eyes were some of the first tells a gambler looked for during a game. Judging by the outcome of the hand, that breath was most definitely something more than a way to fill the other man's lungs.

As long as he got a look at one of Marland's tells, Clint didn't mind losing a hand along the way. He could more than make up for it now that he knew what to look for throughout the night. Bill hadn't given up much by way of a tell, but then again he hadn't had anything to be happy about either. Like most younger men, he wasn't too good at hiding it when he was disappointed with a draw and once even swore under his breath the moment he fanned his cards.

Things like that were fine in casual games, but had no place around professional players. Of course, the professionals themselves didn't mind such displays at all.

Clint had been watching the Major closest of all. So far, he had yet to spot a single tell. There were a few distinctive coughs or a way he drummed his fingers, but nothing that struck Clint as anything important. And none of those mannerisms were consistent.

As his mind plowed through all this information on its own, Clint was also thinking about what Peter was doing and if the town's law was keeping a good enough eye on him. Clint hated to leave the Englishman alone so soon after the ambush in Peter's shop, but no matter how fast Clint was, even he couldn't be two places at once.

Clint sat in his chair, presenting himself as the perfect picture of relaxation. With more poker games under his belt than he could even guess, Clint had the skill of masking his thoughts down to a fine art. The cards of a fresh hand were dealt and he scooped them up at the same time as everyone else.

The three of hearts, four of diamonds, and nine of spades didn't mean too much to him. The pair of jacks, on the other hand, most definitely caught his eye.

Bill looked through his cards, shaking his head at first before stopping and nodding ever so slightly. The fact that his nod was subtle was probably his way of keeping to himself. The truth of the matter was that he'd just dropped his pants to anyone looking his way.

Clint, of course, had caught the nod and glanced over toward Marland.

The portly man to Clint's right didn't nod and didn't let out that distinctive heavy breath. Knowing he wasn't going to get much else from him for the moment, Clint shifted his gaze straight ahead. "Your bet, Major," he said.

Major Waterman nodded, but only in response to Clint's statement. He didn't do anything that struck Clint as a tell, but he did look mildly annoyed at being reminded of the betting order. "Lord knows why I'm doing this so early, but I'll throw in for thirty-five."

Whatever Clint might have thought of the Major, he figured the man was no slouch of a poker player. Therefore, anything that came out of Waterman's mouth regarding his hand was immediately disregarded in Clint's mind. Words like that were only to clear the throat, break the silence, or mess with the less experienced heads of the game.

Marland paused a second before going for his chips, but threw in enough to call the bet.

Clint counted out his chips and then paused. "I might as well raise five dollars," he said with a casual shrug while tossing in the money.

Bill was only too eager to match the bet. It might have been his way of being sneaky, but he also bumped the bet up another ten. Whatever he had, it must have looked real good to the younger man. He even managed to keep his bright spirits when the Major tossed in enough to keep himself in the game without a moment's hesitation.

Everyone threw back three of their cards and waited for Bill to deal out the replacements. Knowing that the kid with the scars was so proud of a pair, Clint thought even less of the young man's poker prowess.

TWENTY-FOUR

As the cards were dealt, Clint kept his eyes and ears open for any trace of a tell from the others. Marland didn't make a sound this time, but that hardly mattered since he folded as soon as the Major tossed out fifteen dollars' worth of chips.

Clint got an ace and king of spades, which looked nice next to his jacks but didn't mean a hell of a lot. The seven of clubs meant even less.

Just looking at Bill, however, was more than enough to convince Clint that the kid had added something good to his pair. The kid with the scars did a lousy job of holding back a gleeful yelp as he fanned out his new hand of cards.

Deciding that this was as good a time as any to test his ability to judge character, Clint nodded and let a smirk drift over his face as he looked at Bill. "I'll see the fifteen and raise another fifteen."

Bill thought it over for a full second before adding his own chips to the pot. "Why the hell not? And add on another twenty."

"I'll tell you why the hell not," Major Waterman said to the youngest player at the table. "Because I doubt I can beat whatever it is that's got you so proud of yourself."

With that, he folded his cards into a neat pile and set them
on top of the rest of the discards.

Clint nodded to the Major to acknowledge the play and
turned to face Bill. When he stared across the table at the
younger man, he set his face into a rigid, determined
mask. There was nothing about his expression that could
be mistaken for anything but pure business. Apart from
that, Clint tinted his features with just enough smug su-
periority for even the kid to catch.

"I see your twenty," Clint said, "And raise fifty more."

Bill's eyes reflexively widened at the bet and he looked
down at his cards. Staring down at them, he straightened
them in his hand and moved his eyes back and forth over
the painted paper as if the cards themselves were his only
council.

Watching the kid's every movement without moving
his eyes away from Bill's face, Clint noticed that the cards
in Bill's hand were now situated so that one of them could
barely be seen from behind the others. That pretty much
told Clint that the kid was only interested in looking at
four of the five cards and that could only mean two things:
two pair or four of a kind.

If Clint was right, the kid had him beat either way. All
that remained was to test the younger man's guts.

Finally, Bill pushed in all of his remaining chips and
said, "Your fifty, plus twenty-three more."

"See that and raise you another fifty."

This time, the expression on Bill's face was unmistakable anger. His eyes darted down to the cards in his hand
and his fingers began to tighten around them. Just as it
looked like he might pitch the cards across the room, Bill
was stopped short by a voice from right beside him.

"I've got you covered, kid," Major Waterman said. "Go
on and play your hand. But don't waste my money, Bill.
That wouldn't be good for you at all."

"All right, then," Bill said cautiously. "I'll raise another
. . . twenty."

"And another seventy-five on top of it," Clint fired back

without batting an eye. Smiling, he said, "Can't fault me for taking advantage of someone with such deep pockets."

Bill no longer seemed concerned about even trying to maintain a straight face. Instead, he seemed much more concerned with the man to his left. The Major was staring at him intently; his face as cold and unreadable as something etched in stone.

"What'll it be, Bill?" Clint asked right when he felt the younger man's nerves were about to snap. "Care to throw any more of the Major's money my way?"

Bill looked up at Clint and then back down at his cards. He looked from his cards and then up at the Major. From there, he looked back to his cards, back to Waterman, and then once more to his hand.

Watching all of this as though he was sitting in the audience of a theater, Clint kept his eyes fixed right on Bill and didn't let them move for a moment. When he saw that the kid could only look at him for a fraction of a second at a time, he knew what Bill's answer would be even before the words came from that nervous, scarred face.

"Fold," Bill said bitterly, tossing his cards down hard enough for them to land face-up upon the table.

The kid had been holding a pair of queens as well as a pair of kings. Even with one of those pairs, he could have beaten Clint's jacks. But the cards were only a part of the game. Poker was as much a test of a man's character as it was his luck.

Bill, it seemed, had neither.

TWENTY-FIVE

Clint pretended not to pay attention to Bill's cards and instead placed his facedown in front of him. Raking in the chips, Clint made a manageable stack while Major Waterman gathered up all the cards to be shuffled and dealt again. Before the first card landed in front of Marland, Clint pushed away from the table and got to his feet.

"You're not leaving, are you," the Major asked. Judging by the look in his eyes, however, the words were more of a statement of fact rather than any kind of question.

Clint shrugged and stretched his back. "I just need to excuse myself for a moment. Nature calls." He started to head toward the closest door and then stopped to turn back to the table. "Should I take my chips with me?"

If the Major seemed somewhat agitated before, he appeared downright angered by that last question. "Your chips will be fine, Adams. You're free to take them if you don't trust us well enough."

Just to get under the Major's skin one more time, Clint made it look as though he was seriously considering his options before shrugging. "I guess everything should be alright where it is," he said before heading once again for the door.

Clint only caught a glimpse of Major Waterman's face before he turned around, but that was enough for him to catch the flash of rage behind the other man's eyes. It was one of the few times that Clint had been able to elicit a real response from the Major and it made him more than a little proud that he'd been able to break through at all.

It didn't matter what the Major might have done to Peter, Clint had no fear that one of his chips would be missing when he returned. That, if nothing else, was something that simply went without saying. The Double Diamond wouldn't have been able to stay in business at all if that kind of simple security couldn't be guaranteed.

What concerned Clint more was what would happen outside the club. More importantly, he was worried that Peter Banks had been out of his sight for far too long.

The clock inside Clint's brain had been ticking away the seconds ever since he'd stepped out of Doctor Garza's office. Sending the deputy over to keep an eye on the Englishman did something to ease Clint's nerves, but was in no way intended to be a permanent solution. The law would be little help at best. Someone trying to steal a project funded by the U.S. government would have come up with a way to work around the law before making their first move.

And if they didn't plan on working around the law, they would certainly be prepared to cut through it.

Just thinking along those lines caused Clint to pick up his pace. The back door of the club led out to a small lot that was filled up mostly by a walk-in outhouse. The outhouse was a medium-sized shed that was built to accommodate several people at once. There was a smaller shed on the other part of the lot which was set aside for the ladies.

Clint veered away sharply from both sheds as soon as he heard the door to the club slam shut behind him. Since there was nobody to see him, he jogged around the main building and headed for the boardwalk in front of the Double Diamond. Clint hopped up onto the walkway and took a quick look around.

Traffic on James Street had picked up considerably in

the time Clint had been inside the gambling club. It was
only late afternoon but thanks to the shorter winter days,
the sun was already sinking in the sky. Darkness was still
a ways off, but the day had taken a turn for the colder
and the air felt like needles prickling against Clint's exposed skin.

It was hard to tell if the snow drifting through the air
was falling from the clouds or was being blown off the
rooftops. Either way, it added yet another texture to the
breeze which wandered among the people passing by on
horseback, in wagons, or on foot. None of those people
seemed out of place in Clint's mind, so he moved down
the street in the direction of Doctor Garza's office.

Now, along with the clock in his head that had been
running this entire time, Clint was keeping track of the
time he'd been away from the card table as well. He knew
it wouldn't take long for Major Waterman to become suspicious about Clint's absence, but if too much time went
by that could force the situation a little further than it
needed to go.

For the moment, Clint still felt pretty safe about the
amount of time that had passed. He was making good
progress down the street and could already see the storefront marked by a shingle bearing the doctor's name. Clint
was about to cross the street and head into the office when
a sound caught his attention.

That sound came from behind him and the only reason
Clint had noticed was because it stopped immediately
when his own steps had halted. There wasn't a lot of time
to waste, so Clint spun around and looked over his shoulder at the street he'd just covered.

Standing there, not even trying to blend into their sur-
roundings, was a pair of bulky figures keeping their shoulders squared and their heads down to avoid the rays of
the sun. Both of the men were armed with pistols carried
in holsters around their waists and both of them were staring directly at Clint.

Seeing those two behind him came as no surprise to

Clint. On the contrary, he would have been more surprised if he hadn't been followed. Surely, the pair behind him had made their presence known to make Clint uneasy. They had their thumbs hooked through their gun belts and a scowl on their faces that caused the other locals to give them a wide berth as they passed by.

Clint was unimpressed. Once he'd spotted them, he turned back around and went straight to the door to Garza's office. It opened easily, allowing Clint to move inside.

The doctor was sitting at his rolltop desk and one of his beds was occupied by a figure stretched out beneath a thick blanket. The deputy was nowhere to be found, however, and neither was Peter.

TWENTY-SIX

"Where's Peter?" Clint asked, charging into the doctor's office and taking another look around. "What happened?"

The man resting on the bed in the back of the room looked more than a little stunned at the sight of Clint barging through the front door like an angry bull. All that Clint was concerned about, however, was the fact that the man in that bed looked nothing like Peter Banks.

Doctor Garza stood up and held out both hands in a calming manner. "Nothing happened, Mister Adams. Just settle down."

"And what about the deputy I asked to come over here? Did he even bother to show up?"

"He was here and he stayed right up until Peter decided to leave."

That hit Clint in the face like a bucketful of cold water. "What? Peter decided to leave?"

Garza nodded. "That's right." Checking a silver watch he removed from his pocket, he added, "About an hour ago."

"And you let him?"

"There wasn't much more for me to do and besides, there wasn't much I could do to prevent him from going once he'd set his mind to it. If you know Peter at all, you can understand what I mean."

Clint took a breath and forced himself to calm down. Hearing what the doctor had said brought a bunch of memories flooding into Clint's mind. "Sorry if I snapped at you, Doc," Clint said. "If Peter got it in his mind to go, it would have taken a team of mules pulling the other direction to keep him from leaving."

"I see you do know him pretty well, after all," Doctor Garza said with a smirk. "Believe me, I tried to keep him here."

When he glanced back toward the single occupied bed, Clint found the man staring back at him with wide, frightened eyes. The blanket was almost pulled completely over his head.

"Sorry for the scare," Clint said to the man in the sickbed. "I'll be going now." Clint turned to leave, but stopped once he'd stepped a little closer to the doctor. "Do you know where he went?"

"He was in a damned rush to get out of here and when I tried to talk him out of it, he said he'd check in with me later and was gone before I could say another word."

"At least tell me the deputy was still with him."

"He wasn't hot on Peter's heels, but I sent him out of here to follow him. It all happened so fast, that was the best I could do."

"It sounds like you did everything you could, Doc. Thanks a lot."

"Do you think Peter might still be in trouble?"

A lot of things went through Clint's mind at that moment, but not one of them was that Peter was anywhere close to being free and clear of this mess he was in. But rather than make the doctor feel any worse about the situation, Clint tried to look as relaxed as possible. "Probably not. These things have a way of looking a lot worse than they are."

Doctor Garza smiled nervously. "You have a good poker face, but what you say doesn't exactly match with the way you came charging in here. I'll keep an eye out for him and get word to you if I find him."

"That would be much appreciated. I'm staying at the Double Diamond."

"Fine. Now get going. Suddenly, I want to know how Peter is doing every bit as much as you do."

Normally, Clint might think he was easily more concerned for the Englishman since he knew exactly what was going on. There was something about the doctor, however, that said Garza truly did care as much as he said.

After a quick nod and another hasty apology to the man lying in the sickbed, Clint was out the door and heading down the boardwalk. He didn't know the town of Gemmell as well as he would have liked, but Clint was awfully familiar with the way Peter Banks's mind worked. If there was a wager to be made, Clint would have bet everything that the Englishman went straight back to his workshop as soon as he left the doctor.

Clint kept his eyes and ears open for any sign that he was being followed. He didn't even walk ten paces before he caught a glimpse of those two figures following him. Since one of those figures wasn't Bill with the scars on his face, Clint checked off another two of Major Waterman's men that were accounted for.

That left two or three that were healthy and moving around somewhere outside of Clint's perception. Normally, those weren't too horrible of odds. On the other hand, those two gunmen could also be pulling a trigger on Peter at that very moment and if that happened, Clint wouldn't be able to look at himself in a mirror.

All Clint could do at the moment was put the darker possibilities to the back of his mind so he could focus on what he could do. It wasn't helping Peter at all for Clint to fret about all the things that could go wrong. In fact, that wasn't even in Clint's nature to think that way. It was at that moment when Clint realized just how important Peter was to him.

Peter had been a friend, teacher, and even mentor to

Clint. Peter Banks had had a lot to do with the man that Clint turned out to be.

As he sped down the street with those other two trailing behind him, Clint let out a breath and calmed his nerves with a solid, intense effort. He steeled himself in much the same way he'd done when playing cards with Major Waterman only minutes ago. Emotion had to be set aside along with anything else that would divert any part of himself from what needed to be done.

When he drew in his next breath, Clint narrowed his focus onto one particular goal and nothing else.

He would help Peter Banks any way that he could.

Everything might not go exactly according to Clint's plan and he might not make the perfect decision at every turn, but Clint was going to do everything possible to accomplish that goal.

It was a simple thing to do, but it made Clint feel more in control of the trail he was riding. His mind no longer felt like it was rattling around inside his head. There was a job to do. Pure and simple.

All that remained was to do it.

TWENTY-SEVEN

Peter didn't live in his shop. In fact, there was an entire town full of places for Peter to go after leaving Doctor Garza's office. Even though Clint knew that, there was no doubt in his mind that he would find the Englishman hard at work in his own place of business.

There wasn't enough time to worry about the men following him. Clint had to get to Peter as soon as possible. That was the goal and there was nothing more important within Clint's mind.

It seemed as though the walk to Peter's shop was taking an eternity. Clint felt as though he'd taken enough steps to circle the entire town at least twice, but the familiar storefront was only just coming into view. His brain thinking several steps ahead, Clint plotted out his entrance through the back lot as he was physically just approaching the fence behind the shop.

As Clint opened the gate and stepped into the makeshift shooting range, he was planning how he would search every inch of the shop's interior if he couldn't spot Peter right away. That particular plan was completely unnecessary, however, since Peter was right where Clint thought he would be.

The Englishman wasn't moving anywhere close to his normal speed, but he was still shuffling from one bench to another, hefting pieces of metal in both hands. Unlike when Clint had first been in that workshop, every surface was covered with bits and pieces of dismantled weaponry and the smell of gun oil was heavy in the air.

"Hello, there," Peter said cheerily. "One of the undertaker's sons came by to collect that body, so I didn't see any harm in getting back to work. You never brought my gin."

"You didn't see any harm?" Clint asked. "What about the harm that almost came to you the last time you were in this same room? I suppose you forgot all about that."

"I couldn't forget about that, Clint. But I also can't let that unpleasantness keep me from my appointed task. Surely, you can't be suggesting that I go into hiding for the rest of my life."

After making sure the back door to the workshop was locked, Clint stepped over to a small, narrow window that looked out onto the shooting range. The window was covered by a strip of thick burlap and was held in place by a couple hooks which fit through the material.

"I'm not suggesting you give up your work," Clint said while looking out for any sign of the men that had been following him. "I am suggesting that you lay low for a little while since the blood on your floor is still fresh. Hell, Peter, you took a bullet yourself. Don't you think that's reason enough to be cautious?"

Peter reached down with his right hand to pat a holster that was strapped around his waist. "I am being cautious. Until I feel safe, I won't be going anywhere without arming myself. In case you haven't noticed, I'm not a bad shot. I don't need a nursemaid."

"And I wasn't saying you did need one. All I'm saying is that you need to keep your wits about you." Even as the words came out of his mouth, Clint knew he'd said them wrong. Part of him almost expected the older man to backhand him for speaking out of turn. The other part of him wanted to backhand Peter for being too stubborn to admit that he was in serious jeopardy.

"I can take care of myself." Peter said in a stern tone.
"If you think I'm so helpless, then why don't you come
over here and try to make me leave my shop before I'm
damn good and ready?"

"You know I hold you in high regard. But someone
had to come and drag a dead body out of this very room.
Those men were here thinking it was going to be your
body being dragged out of here. And just so you know,
there were a couple men following me just now who more
than likely have that same idea in their heads."

"Really? Is that what you're looking out that window
for?"

"Yep."

"And are they out there?"

Clint took another look through the glass pane and
scanned the lot behind the gun shop. Even though the
window itself was small, it was possible to see just about
all of the lot through it. Holding back the burlap with one
hand, Clint looked outside and then looked again.

The lot was empty.

For a moment, Clint seriously considered lying to Peter
just to convince the other man to get the hell out of that
building. As much as he would have been justified in doing that, he simply couldn't bring himself to manipulate
his friend in such a way.

Finally, Clint let out a low grumbling sigh and said,
"No. There's nobody out there right now. But that doesn't
mean they won't be coming."

Peter dismissed the threat with a quick wave and turned
around to what he'd been doing. "I know I'm in danger,
Clint. I'd have to be a twit not to know something like
that. But what I'm doing is too important for me to be
scared away right now.

"I'm not a young man anymore and if I let myself get
sidetracked from this, I may never be able to get back to
it before someone else finishes up what I've started."

"Can I at least convince you to move your work to

another place? There's got to be somewhere else you can set up for just a little while."

"I'm too close right now and packing everything up would only break my train of thought. Besides, if those men really are outside, we'd only be delivering this project straight into their hands."

At that moment, Clint was fully convinced that there was no way short of him physically dragging the Englishman out of there that Peter was going to move from his spot. He could talk until he was blue in the face, but Clint knew damn well that once Peter had his mind set on something, there was nothing in heaven or earth that would change it. In a strange, frustrating way, that was another trait that Clint and Peter had in common.

Knowing only too well what it was like to be stubborn as a mule, Clint pulled the burlap off the window completely so he could look through it from just about any where in the room. "All right," he said. "Let's see what this important project of yours really is."

Peter's face lit up like the Fourth of July. "I was hoping you'd ask. Once you get a look at this, you'll see the method to my madness."

TWENTY-EIGHT

For the next couple of minutes, Clint was beginning to wonder if he would ever truly see the method to Peter's madness. As time went by, he did become more and more convinced that the Englishman most definitely had some kind of madness going on.

Peter shuffled from one side of the room to another, taking one piece of metal and moving it to another bench. From there, he would go to another rack in the workshop where he would find yet another piece. A wooden stock was taken from a small vice bolted to yet another table until finally one workbench was practically brimming with materials.

Just as Clint was about to ask what was going on, he noticed the pieces coming together under Peter's flying hands. Once the Englishman stayed in one place, he began assembling the pieces he'd collected until something finally began to take shape.

At first, the thing looked like some kind of oversized grinder. Then, it looked like a large pistol. Before too much longer, it resembled more of a rifle. When he was finally done, Peter hefted the contraption in his arms and held it out like a proud father.

"Well?" Peter said. "What do you think?"

Clint was speechless. All he could do was let his eyes

wander back and forth over the odd-shaped gun in an effort to soak it all in. The barrel was actually a collection of barrels wrapped up in a tight bundle and held together by metal rings. Now Clint recognized the comparison Peter had been making earlier to Gatling guns. Although this weapon did resemble a Gatling, the scale had been sized down drastically.

The barrels were each a little over a foot long and appeared to be wide enough to fire nothing bigger than a .38-caliber round. Behind the barrels was a trigger which harkened back to a pistol or even a rifle. Upon closer examination, Clint could see there were actually two triggers side by side much like a double-barreled shotgun.

The wooden grip had looked similar to a rifle grip, but not once it had been attached to the rest of the assembly. Although it was obviously carved to conform to someone's hand up close to the triggers, the grip tapered off and thinned out as it went back. A couple inches back from the trigger, a slender metal band emerged from the grip and curved slightly inward.

These were all the parts that Clint could immediately identify. Besides that, there was some kind of exposed mechanism in the middle of the gun where a cylinder might be. There was also a rectangular hole above and below the trigger housing.

"Well?" Peter asked again. "Are you going to give me your opinion, or do I need to complete this on my own?"

"I've seen plenty of guns in my time," Clint said. "I've stripped them down and put them back together, but I've never seen anything like this. I barely know what I'm looking at."

"Would you care for a demonstration?"

"Yeah. I sure would."

Like a child showing off his newest toy, Peter turned around and fetched a few more pieces from the nearest bench. One of the pieces was a metal container which fit tightly into the rectangular hole on top of the gun. The other piece looked like a simple crank handle and that fit into the side where a cylinder would normally be.

"This," Peter said while tapping the metal container sticking out of the top of the gun, "holds the ammunition."

".38 caliber?" Clint asked.

The Englishman smiled proudly. "Right you are. This box can hold thirty rounds and gravity feeds it through. There's a bit of a jamming problem as you might imagine, but that will all be ironed out in time."

Actually, Clint couldn't quite imagine the jamming problem but he decided to let Peter continue his explanation uninterrupted.

"It fits over your arm like so." As he said that, Peter slid his forearm along the inside of the grip and slid his finger over the trigger. He used his free hand to move the metal band so that it curled around his elbow and snapped into place once it wrapped around to meet up with the grip from the other side. The end of the band slid into a notch carved into the wooden grip. "This will be adjustable in the final model as well, but for now it's tailored for me."

Now that Clint had had a moment to soak in the sight of the thing, he was beginning to wrap his mind around it a bit more. The gunsmith part of his brain was stretching out and taking over inside of him, pushing back the part that had only wanted to deal with whoever might be looking over his shoulder.

"You were mentioning Gatling guns before," Clint pointed out. "Is that what that crank on the side is for?"

"Partially. Ready for a demonstration?"

TWENTY-NINE

"That thing is ready to be fired? It looks kind of . . ." Clint paused before saying the first words that had sprung to mind. "Well . . . it looks kind of pieced together. I thought it was just a model."

"It is pieced together, but it is also a working model. I just don't think it can hold up to repeated uses. Let's give it a go, shall we?" And with that, Peter was off. He didn't even wait for a response from Clint before he strode across the room and unlocked the door leading to the back lot.

Clint tried to stop the Englishman from going outside, but he simply wasn't fast enough to pull off the task. Besides that, he wasn't all too eager to jump in front of a man with a miniature cannon strapped to his forearm.

Peter stepped outside and took up his position at one end of the lot. In front of him at the other end was the wooden rack set up to hold targets ranging from paper outlines to a row of bottles. Currently, the only thing there was the bull's-eye painted upon the wood itself.

By the look on the Englishman's face, he was simply in the midst of another day at work. If he had actually heard any of the things Clint had warned him about, his face didn't show the slightest hint. Rather than so much as look around for any unwanted visitors, Peter was fidgcting with the contraption on his arm, making several last-minute adjustments.

Clint followed the Englishman out and felt his nerves immediately tense up. He scanned the lot for those two men and even strained his ears for the sound of footsteps or any other indication that they were not alone in the vicinity of the lot.

As far as Clint could tell, there wasn't anyone about to storm through the gate. Since Peter was dead-set on going through his motions, Clint took what little comfort he could in that and made sure he was ready to deal with anyone who did try and ambush them.

"All right, Clint," Peter said as he raised his left arm up to the crank sticking out of the side of the gun. Wincing slightly as the motion pulled at his wound, he said, "Let's give this a go. You might want to stand behind me."

Clint moved around so he could stand behind and to the right of the Englishman. Peter watched him the entire time and didn't take his eyes away until Clint was in a spot he considered to be safe.

Taking hold of the crank, Peter lifted the gun so it was pointed toward the painted bull's-eye and planted his feet squarely at shoulder width apart. He turned the crank much like he would a small blender, which set the barrels into motion.

Much like a Gatling gun, the ring of barrels began to rotate. Unlike the Gatling, nothing happened as the barrels moved around. Nothing happened, that is, until the barrels were coming around for their second revolution.

Clint jumped slightly as the first shot was fired. The report was slightly louder than normal and caused the gun to jump in Peter's hand. That shot was followed by another and then another, popping off again and again, chewing away bits of the wooden target with every blast.

The speed of the shots got faster until they sounded very much like the chatter of a Gatling gun. There wasn't the same amount of power behind every shot, but it was damn close. The biggest difference came as Peter kept turning the crank until the gun was easily firing faster than a Gatling.

As he emptied the ammunition crate, filling the air with smoke and rolling thunder, Peter was smiling wide enough to catch flies in his teeth. His muscles were straining with the effort of holding the gun in line with the target and his legs even seemed to be fighting to keep himself from being knocked backward. But even with all that work, he looked as though he'd never been happier.

The target at the other end of the lot was reduced to a plank of gnawed wood. A couple more shots knocked even that to the ground as round after round punched holes through the gate behind where the target had been.

Clint's ears were ringing and his nerves were jumping beneath his skin. He felt a kind of jitteriness that normally only came on a battlefield as shots were coming from all directions. With the sheer amount of lead being thrown about, he realized that one gun like that might actually stand a chance against a small regiment of soldiers.

The shots finally subsided, followed by a rattle as Peter gave the crank one more turn. In front of him, the gate and what was left of the target stand looked as though it had been torn apart by a dozen firing squads.

"Overheating is still a bit of a problem as well," Peter shouted over the ringing in both his and Clint's ears. "But that's just another thing that will be ironed out in time. Here's another benefit of my creation over the Gatling gun."

As he said that, Peter took hold of the crank and pulled back on it. There was a metallic clank and then the crank moved freely in the opposite direction. Two cranks was all it took before there was another clank which caused Peter to smile proudly.

The Englishman twisted his arm until he held the gun sideways. From that position, the metal container that held the ammunition fell off and dropped to the ground. Still grinning like a proud poppa, Peter reached behind him and pulled another similar metal container from where it had been hooked to his belt. That container was snapped into place and locked down in a matter of seconds.

For a few moments, Peter stood with his arm pointed toward the ground and the gun hanging from it like some bulky, iron tentacle. He and Clint looked at each other without saying a word, both men waiting for the ringing in their ears to die down enough for them to hear.

Clint looked back and forth between the obliterated target rack and fence and the gun strapped to Peter's hand which still spewed black smoke. Before too long, Clint could hear the wind blowing through the lot and then he could hear the sound of Peter's voice.

"Now that," the Englishman said proudly, "is what I call the devil's spark."

THIRTY

When he got back inside Peter's workshop, Clint went over to a stove built into the middle of the room and started building a fire within its black iron belly. There was a biting chill in the air which Clint had felt the moment they'd stepped outside. But there was something else that sent another kind of shiver down his spine.

It was that gun which Peter seemed to regard as his one and only child. Now that Clint had seen that little Gatling spit out enough lead to drop over a dozen men, he felt his stomach shrink around a cold, icy pit.

Peter, on the other hand, couldn't have removed the smile from his face with a crowbar.

"Tell me," the Englishman said. "Tell me what you think. I've been waiting to hear your opinion since you arrived in town. There are still a few things to be worked out as I mentioned, but even at this stage of its development, this piece has got to be one of the most impressive I've ever worked on."

"There's no doubt it's impressive," Clint said. "Who did you say is funding all of this?"

"It's a government contract. I believe it will be taken by the army once I'm done ironing out all the wrinkles." Holding up his arm, Peter gazed down at the gun still strapped to it and turned it over so he could look at all

117

sides. "I've already come up with ideas to streamline the design. I'm thinking of curving the ammunition boxes so they're not quite so cumbersome. Did you see how fast it was to reload?"

"Yeah. I saw."

"So what do you think?"

Clint had to wait before he answered. There were so many things running through his head that he barely even knew where to begin. "Look," he said finally. "I know that you take your work seriously and that you have the best intentions at heart."

Peter's eyes narrowed and his smile started to fade. "Then why do I sense the phrase 'road to hell' coming up?"

Shrugging, Clint balanced his words once more before speaking them. He decided that Peter had earned the right to hear exactly what was on his mind. "Well . . . would I be so far off?"

"Bloody right, you would be! What kind of a man do you take me for?"

"That's not the question, Peter. The question here is what kind of a man is the one you'll be handing over that gun of yours to once all the kinks are ironed out?"

"I told you who they were."

"And are you absolutely sure they're with the government? And even if they are, are you sure they need to have a weapon like this?"

"I'm not sure I follow you."

Now, more than ever, Clint saw the difference between himself and Peter. The difference hadn't been so great when he'd been learning from the Englishman, but now that Clint had spent more time out in the world, that difference had become like a canyon between them.

Peter was an expert at what he did. He fixed guns, built them, even created them. He did all of that inside a shop that he rarely ever left.

Clint learned a trade as well, but he did a lot more than fix and clean guns. He fired them and had them fired at him as well. Throughout the course of that life, Clint had come to know plenty of other men who lived by their guns and most of them were not very nice.

Thinking about the kind of men that would practically salivate over the chance to get their hands on a gun like the one on Peter's hand sent that extra cold chill through Clint's spine. It was only too easy to imagine who would pay to get a gun like that for themselves and what that kind of man would do once he'd gotten it.

"I'm not sure I like the way you're looking at me, Clint," Peter said. "I asked for your opinion. Go ahead and give it to me. We are still friends, aren't we?"

Clint nodded. "Last time I checked."

"Then tell me what's on your mind."

"All right. Why are you doing this?"

Peter was in the midst of removing the gun from his arm and dismantling it piece by piece. "Doing what? This project?"

"Yes. Why are you making something like that and then handing it over to people you hardly know you can trust?"

The Englishman set down the bulk of the weapon and looked it over. He then looked up at Clint with confusion spread all over his face. "Because this is what I do. What kind of a question is that? Are you saying I should feel guilty because I make weapons? Because if you are, I'd have to remind you that you're in the same trade. In fact, you use your weapon a hell of a lot more than I use mine."

"That's true, but I know who my weapon is being used against. And even so, nothing I've ever used . . . or even seen . . . can cause the amount of destruction that thing there is capable of."

Some of the confusion melted away, only to be replaced by a look of tired resignation. "I see. This is an ethical question."

"If you want to look at it that way, then yes. It is about ethics."

"I suppose the next thing you'll ask me is if I feel it's

morally right to manufacture guns, knowing that they'll
only be used to kill other people."

"Well," Clint said carefully. "Something like that gun
isn't exactly made for hunting rabbits."

"No, it isn't. It's made for gunning down a line of men,
which in case you'd forgotten, is the way wars are won."
Now Peter was getting angry. The fact that it showed at
all upon the normally reserved Englishman's face told
Clint that there was plenty more emotion that he wasn't
able to see.

"I know what I do for a living, Clint. You don't have
to remind me about that. But if you want me to feel guilty
for upgrading our nation's military and giving us an advantage on the battlefield, then you're not going to find
any of that here."

"This is exactly what I'd wanted to avoid—"

"Then you have a strange way of avoiding it," Peter
interrupted.

"But now that I've said it, let me also say that I think
you've made a hell of an accomplishment. And since
you're already mad at me, let me just say that you need
to be careful who gets their hands on this accomplishment
because it could cause some major problems if it falls into
the wrong hands.

"You're a good man, Peter, and I would never think
you'd do anything to intentionally hurt anyone. This craft
. . . our craft . . . is necessary. But you can be naive sometimes and a little too quick to trust someone who knows
the right things to say."

Once again, anger flashed in Peter's eyes, but it faded
away almost immediately. Rather than shout back with
any kind of retort, he lowered his head and nodded
slowly. "I understand what you mean."

"Then you should also understand that I think nothing
but the best of you. You're open and honest, but there's
plenty of folks out there who would take advantage of
that in a heartbeat if that meant they could get a hold of
something half as good as that devil's spark you created."

Stepping forward, Clint put his hand on Peter's shoulder. "I know a lot about dealing with skunks. Just trust me when I tell you that I'm smelling one every time you talk about whoever is paying for this contract."

Peter had been returning to his normal self and looked as though he was about to extend his hand in friendship when suddenly his manner changed. The hand that had been coming up to shake Clint's now shot down to the bench in front of him and started frantically fitting pieces of the gun back together.

Clint's nerves immediately tensed when he saw that Peter was racing to get the gun back onto his forearm. "What's the matter?" Clint asked.

"Those skunks you were talking about," the Englishman said as his eyes darted toward the back door. "I think I just saw one of them skulking about."

THIRTY-ONE

Clint didn't have to hear another word before he turned and dashed toward the door leading to the lot behind Peter's shop. Already, he could imagine those two familiar figures that had been following him making their way through the alley on their way to another ambush. Clint looked through the window next to the door, searching for a hint of what had spooked Peter so much.

Although he couldn't see anything moving right away, Clint wasn't going to take any chances and flattened his back against the wall beside the window. "Peter," he said in a tone sharp enough to command his friend's attention. "Get away from there and take cover. It's not safe to—"

Before Clint could finish his warning, the glass next to him exploded inward a split second after a shot ripped through the air just outside the door. Glass sprayed inside the workshop and lead hissed through the air. More shots were already being fired from outside, causing Clint to slide down the wall until he was crouching with his chin tucked tightly against his chest.

Before he looked at what was coming from outside, Clint looked inside the workshop to check one last time on Peter. The Englishman had dropped to his knees and was gathering up all the pieces of his new gun in his arms. Even as the shots kept whipping through the air, Peter

122

made sure he had every last scrap of metal before ducking under the closest table.

Clint didn't even have to think about drawing the Colt before his pistol was in his hand and ready to be fired. Still keeping himself low, he waited for the shots to die down a bit before chancing a look through the window.

It was only a matter of seconds, but it seemed as though an hour had gone by before the roar of gunshots tapered off even slightly. Not only was the glass in the window-pane all but knocked out, but there were holes through the door and wall as well. There were even a few holes punched through the wood not too far above Clint's head.

It was obvious the shooters weren't taking any chances this time around. It was also obvious that they intended on getting what they came for even if it meant killing every living thing within the shop along the way.

Thinking that, Clint's mind flashed to the main show-room of the shop and if there was anybody in there who might be in danger. The next thing that moved through his head was a warning about who else might be walking through that very same showroom.

Without letting another moment slip by, Clint hurried through the workshop, making sure to keep his head low and the rest of him away from the back door and window. He moved around the perimeter of the workshop until he'd positioned himself against the wall next to one of the many benches that were scattered throughout the clut-tered space.

The bench came up past Clint's waist level and was made of thick, chipped lumber. Its top was covered with various tools and scrap bits of wood and steel. There were even a few pistols among the stuff, but Clint wasn't in-terested in any of that. Instead, he put his shoulders against the side of the bench and planted his feet against the floor.

When he pushed the first time, Clint didn't think he'd even be able to budge the workbench. Not only was the thing heavy as hell, but it probably hadn't been moved

from its spot since it was first put there when Peter opened
the shop for business how ever many years ago.

Clint's blood was pounding through his veins, giving
him enough extra strength to move the bench on his second try. Once the bulky furniture was moving, it slid
across the floor a little easier. Clint took advantage of his
momentum and kept pushing even though his legs and
back were already starting to feel the strain.

More shots blasted through the workshop, still coming
from the rear window and door. Nobody had kicked down
that back door, however, which made Clint all the more
certain that he was doing the right thing.

Another shove or two and the bench would be in front
of the door leading to the showroom. Knowing that his
time was quickly running out, Clint took a deep breath
and shoved once more using every bit of strength he had
and stretching his legs as far out as they could go.

"Watch how far you push that," Peter shouted as he
raced to get the last pieces of the gun fit back into place.
"You'll cut us off before we can get through the door."

"I know what I'm doing," Clint said, trying to keep his
voice down. He pushed the last bit using just his shoulders
and arms, but that was enough to get the bench where he
wanted it. The bulky lump of wood was now against the
door, blocking all but the hinges.

With that done, Clint ran from the bench and retraced
his steps around the perimeter of the room. Peter was just
about to ask another question when suddenly the door to
the showroom was thrown open, only to be stopped as it
knocked solidly against the bench.

"What the . . . ?" Peter stammered.

Clint grinned as he saw the door rattle against the
bench. Judging by the way it opened and closed and the
profuse swearing that followed, whoever was on the other
side wanted to get through awfully bad. The bullets that
started punching through the door also told Clint something about who was out there.

"Whoever is out back," Clint said. "they were trying to

herd us toward the front of the shop. We would have been caught in a cross fire the moment that door opened."

Peter was grinning as well, but his was more of an expression of relief. He flinched as the shooting intensified and huddled down a little further under the table. The shots were being fired blind, however, and whipped randomly throughout the workshop.

"If I ever doubt your expertise again," Peter said as he reached with one arm for something on top of the table, "just be sure to give me a good knock on the head."

THIRTY-TWO

Clint held his position against the wall at a spot where he could see both sides of the workshop. "I'll do that. For now, though, get ready to move when I tell you and make sure you don't leave any of that gun behind."

"What are you planning, Clint?"

"I was planning on going through that door. Those men out back still think they're pushing us forward. They might not be expecting us to come charging right into them."

Having found the last piece that he'd been looking for, Peter set it down onto the floor beside him and quickly cinched the metal band around his elbow. The gun was now locked in place on his arm and he picked up the ammunition box he'd just gotten so he could snap it into place.

"I know something else they won't be expecting," the Englishman said once the gun was ready to fire.

The gunshots had tapered off somewhat and Clint pressed his ear to the rear wall of the room. He couldn't hear much through the wood and the ringing in his ears, but he could definitely hear footsteps approaching the back door.

"Should I get out of the way?" Clint asked.

Peter's answer was a subtle sideways wave with his free

hand. Clint stepped a little closer to the back door, which was the opposite direction Clint thought he was going to move. Before he could ask any questions, Clint saw the Englishman move out from beneath his table, get to his feet and lift the crank-gun.

Aiming toward the section of wall that was now empty since Clint had moved the bench to block the door, Peter squared his shoulders and braced himself with one leg behind the other. He began turning the crank of the gun slowly at first, but sped up as soon as the bullets started feeding into the rotating barrels.

If Clint thought the sound of the gun was loud outside, it was painfully so within the confines of the workshop. If he didn't know any better, he might have guessed that the room was being ripped apart by an earthquake as shots from the crank-gun blended into a continuous torrent. He covered his ears and shielded his eyes against the acrid smoke and sparks that filled the air.

Clint thought that Peter intended to clear a path through the attackers coming through the back door. Instead, the Englishman had a different agenda and had aimed at a different spot entirely. Now that he could see where Peter was aiming, Clint realized what the Englishman was trying to do.

Peter gritted his teeth as he kept turning that crank. He was aiming at the wall near the floor at first and had steadily moved his arm up, over and back down again. Splinters of wood flew in every direction as hole after hole was punched through the wall where the bench had been.

Knowing that he was reaching the bottom of his ammunition supply, Peter turned the crank even faster, retracing the pattern that he'd so carefully made. When he was finished, he pulled the crank in the opposite direction, dropping the empty ammunition box to the floor.

Clint had been looking out the window for any sign of the shooters. Not surprisingly, they'd stopped where they were once the inside of the shop exploded with gunfire. When he looked back at what Peter had done, Clint saw that the bullet holes formed a rough arch shape through the wall that was just under waist high

"Look to your right," Peter said as he stepped forward and moved toward the damaged wall. "There should be another ammunition box or two on the bench there."

Clint did what he was told and found only one of the metal cases. He picked it up and tossed it to Peter as the Englishman passed by.

With a stiff, downward kick, Peter bashed in the wall within the section he'd outlined in holes. Clint joined in as well and between the two of them, they managed to knock out a chunk of the wall that had been perforated by several dozen well-placed shots.

Clint shook his head in wonder as the piece of wall fell outward. "If the military doesn't want this, you might want to go into the construction business. That's one hell of a saw."

"Construction, my arse. The only reason that worked so well is that I built this workshop as an add-on to my shop and knew it wouldn't take much to punch through. Now get moving before these bastards put me completely out of business."

Dropping to one knee, Clint stuck his head out through the rough opening and looked toward the back of the building. He could hear voices coming from the lot behind the shop but could only make out a few words.

". . . take this side," were the words he could hear. That was enough to let Clint know what was coming next.

"Go on," Clint said as he moved away from the wall. "It sounds like they're splitting up. Get out of here and find someplace safe."

"The restaurant I took you to earlier," Peter said quickly. "Meet me there."

"Will do. Now go."

The Englishman jammed the box of ammunition under his belt and grabbed hold of the ragged edge of the hole he'd created. Ducking his head, he fit easily through the opening, dropped outside and dashed toward the front of the building.

Clint could hear the door to the showroom once again being battered against the bench. This time, the sounds were accompanied by the scraping of the bench's legs against the floor as the piece of furniture was slowly getting pushed aside. It was only a matter of time before someone could fit through that opening and get into the workshop. Long before that, Clint knew the back door would be kicked open as well.

None of that mattered, however, since Clint figured that nobody would be inside the workshop to greet the attackers anyway. After giving Peter enough time to get clear, Clint stuck his head out through the opening in the wall and checked on the Englishman's progress. Peter was already running down the alley and coming out next to the front of his shop.

THIRTY-THREE

Clint forced himself to wait for an additional second before following Peter into the alley. The only reason for that was so he could give the men coming in from the showroom some kind of reception.

The door slammed against the bench once again. This time, there was enough muscle and leverage behind it that it pushed the bench another couple of inches, allowing a pair of men to rush through. The first man to charge into the room did so in an awkward tumble since he almost tripped over the bench that had been blocking the door.

The next man to come through was ready to cover his partner's entrance and fired a couple shots as he came thundering into the workshop. Clint pointed his modified Colt as though he was simply pointing a finger at the other man and then squeezed his trigger. The Colt bucked against his palm and barked once, sending a round through the meaty part of the second man's shoulder.

Having just caught sight of Clint crouching against the wall, that man was just adjusting his aim when the bullet chewed a bloody trench through his shoulder. The impact of the lead knocked him back like he'd been hit with a hammer and his finger tightened reflexively around his own trigger. The bullet slapped into another nearby bench, however, as the man himself staggered back into the showroom.

Clint lined up his back with the hole in the wall and fired off one more shot which gouged a chunk of the bench away that was less than an inch from the first man's waist. Seeing that the bullet had come so close to him was enough to throw the first man even more off balance. It sent him tumbling sideways and over the bench which he'd been trying so desperately to avoid.

When he looked up from his new position on the floor, the first man to charge into the room no longer saw Clint crouching against the wall. In fact, Clint was nowhere to be seen.

Using the Colt's recoil as just a little added momentum, Clint had let himself drop backwards through the hole in the wall as he'd fired that last shot. His shoulders brushed against the jagged edge of the opening and his hat was knocked from his head as he fell out of the workshop.

He tucked his head in close to his chest and hit the ground of the alley shoulders first. The moment Clint felt the impact, he kicked his feet off the shop's floor and pulled his knees in closer to his body so his body could form something of a round shape.

His momentum carried Clint out through the hole, onto the ground and into the alley. There was just enough room between the two buildings for Clint to roll slightly more than one time, which carried him straight into the wall of the neighboring building.

Clint's shoulders and spine smacked against the nearby wall, bringing him to a sudden, jarring halt. He forced his eyes open and fought to see clearly through the dizziness that churned through his head and body. Even though it still felt as though the world was turning around him, Clint managed to pick out one shape that was moving more than all the others.

That shape struck Clint as familiar since it had been one of the bulky figures that had been following him from the Double Diamond all the way to Peter's shop. Clint couldn't hear the gunshot, but he did hear the impact of hot lead into the wall a foot or so over his head. Wood chips dropped down onto his shoulder as he lifted the Colt and let his survival instincts take over from there.

Clint sighted down the Colt's barrel for less than half a second before he pulled his trigger. With his head still spinning from his backward tumble from the building, he couldn't see much more than the figure in front of him jerk back suddenly. Just to be sure, Clint fired once more, dropping the other man flat onto his back.

Shaking the remaining dizziness from his mind, Clint jumped to his feet and took a look around. The closest man to him was the one who'd just been blown off his feet. That one wasn't moving except for the occasional twitch as the pool of blood spread from under his body.

Clint heard a commotion from inside the gun shop as the back door was now kicked in by another of the attackers. Keeping his eye on the hole in the wall, Clint edged toward the mouth of the alley which was where he'd seen Peter heading only moments ago.

He couldn't even catch a glimpse of the Englishman when he got to the front of the alley. There were plenty of folks huddled in nearby doorways, doing their best to keep away from the shooting that had once again come from the small storefront.

Holstering his Colt so he wouldn't spread any more panic, Clint stepped out of the alley and turned his eyes toward the front of Peter's shop. His breath caught in the back of his throat when he spotted someone staring right back at him through the front door which was held open a few inches by a well-placed boot.

THIRTY-FOUR

The man standing in the front door already had his gun raised and was sighting down the barrel when Clint had poked his head around the corner. All he needed to do was pull the trigger, which was exactly what he did once he got a look at Clint's face.

All Clint needed to see was the gun in the man's hand before he threw himself back into the alley. The moment his back hit the wall of the neighboring building, he heard a gunshot explode from Peter's front door. As the bullet punched a hole through the wall where Clint had been standing before, the Colt filled his hand.

Waiting until he heard footsteps pounding against the boardwalk in front of the gun shop, Clint leapt across the alley and flattened his back against the wall of Peter's building. He held the Colt at the ready and turned to look at the boardwalk.

At the first sign of movement coming from that direction, Clint reached out with his left hand and took hold of the other man the moment he turned the corner. Clint's fist closed around the other man's jacket and he used that to pull him into the alley and off his center of gravity. He swung the Colt sharply downward to crack against the other man's wrist, forcing the gunman to let his weapon fall to the ground.

"The others inside," Clint snarled as he tucked the end of the Colt's barrel into the other man's gut. "Call them off."

"Wh . . . what?"

"You heard me!"

But the other man couldn't even get his next words out. More than that, his eyes were filled with a healthy mix of fear and confusion.

Clint slammed the other man against the wall and was about to push his advantage when something caught his eye. What he saw was enough to stop him short and take the Colt from out of the guy's stomach. The metal star pinned to the man's chest had caught a stray beam of daylight which glinted into Clint's face.

"What are you doing here?" Clint asked, trying to keep the same amount of menace in his voice that had been there before.

The deputy couldn't have been more than nineteen years old. He sucked in a breath and looked toward the farthest end of the alley. "We heard the gunshots coming from here. Me and my partner did."

"Was it you that kicked down the door inside or around back?"

"Huh? What doors? We just got here."

Clint backed up a step and pointed at the body lying in the alley. "Is that your partner?"

When the deputy spotted the unmoving figure lying on its back in the dirt, he started to run toward it. He didn't get far before stopping and staring at it a little harder. "No," he said with relief. "That's not him."

Having already picked up the deputy's gun, Clint held it out for the younger man and extended it once the kid turned around. The deputy flinched slightly when he saw that Clint was holding a pistol in each hand. He relaxed again when he saw that not only was one of them his, but it was being offered to him handle-first.

"You don't see too much action in this town do you?" Clint asked.

"Not really."

"Where did your partner go?"

"He went around back. I was just about to bust in through the front when I heard the shooting over this way."

Holding out one arm, Clint used it to push the deputy back with him, flattening them both against the wall. He lowered his voice and watched the hole in the side of the building carefully. "There's going to be more shooting before the day's out. Just be sure to keep your head and watch where you're pointing that gun of yours."

"Is Peter still in there?" the deputy asked.

With the speech he'd given to Peter about trusting folks still fresh in his mind, Clint looked over to study the deputy's face. As much as he hated to admit it, he just didn't know if he could trust this kid just because of the badge pinned to his chest.

"Peter's not in there," Clint told the deputy. "He got away, but we still need to deal with this problem here. Do you know who any of these men are?"

"I haven't even seen any of them except for that dead one over there."

There hadn't been any shooting inside the shop for a while now. Not only that, but the voices and heavy footsteps had tapered off as well. Since Clint knew that it would be too much to ask for the shooters to have snuck away with their tails between their legs, he figured that they were in the process of sneaking up on them.

Clint looked over to the hole that had been shot through the wall and didn't see anyone poking their head through it. Of course, there had been plenty of time for someone to have spotted them while Clint and the deputy were talking. Since he didn't know for sure, Clint assumed the worst.

"Come on," Clint whispered, moving out of the alley and toward the front of the building.

The deputy followed hesitantly which actually made Clint feel a little better about siding with him.

Before Clint walked up the steps leading to the shop's
front door, he pointed toward the deputy and said, "You
stay there. Someone might be coming from the back or
on either side." He didn't wait for a response before moving up to the boardwalk and the door.

Clint walked on the balls of his feet and only stepped
on the edges of the steps so there would be less chance
for a squeak to give him away. The front wall of the shop
was much like most other shops in that it was taken up
mostly by a large picture window for displaying wares.
Although that would allow someone inside to spot Clint,
it also allowed Clint to get a look inside for himself.

The moment he looked through the door, he saw why
nobody had come bursting out through there yet. Inside
the shop, there were three men. Two of the men were
staring intently and pointing their guns at each other.
Their lips were moving, but Clint couldn't hear what they
were saying.

The third man stood in the back of the showroom with
his gun pointed toward the floor. By the look on his face
and the nervous way he shifted from one foot to another,
he wanted to take a shot but was being held in check
somehow.

Clint's first notion was that one of those men had to be
the other deputy. That was the only explanation for the
standoff inside the shop when both Clint and Peter had
already gotten outside. Although this proved to Clint that
the deputies were fighting on the right side, there was still
one major problem.

Both men were standing with their shoulders angled
toward that third man in the back. For that reason, Clint
couldn't see which of them was wearing a badge.

He waited a couple seconds, maneuvering himself so
he couldn't be spotted so easily through the window. That
new angle might have been better for keeping out of sight,
but it only made it harder to see since the glare from the
sun was now washing over the surface of the glass.

If he saw the deputy talking amiably with the other men

or even just walking among them, Clint could have figured the law had thrown in with the attackers. But one of those men in there was outnumbered two to one and about to get hurt. Maybe even killed.

With that in mind, Clint didn't even care if that was the other deputy or not. Someone in there was being held at gunpoint by two killers with itchy trigger fingers. Now all Clint had to do was figure out a way to get into that room quickly without being the spark to set off that powder keg.

Knowing there was no way to move both cautiously and quickly enough to make a difference, Clint chose the lesser of the two evils and didn't look back.

THIRTY-FIVE

The front door of the gun shop exploded inward with one savage kick from Clint's boot. Splinters of all sizes flew in every direction as the door swung in and Clint had entered the room before the door slammed against the wall. He might not have been happy about choosing speed over caution, but since the decision was made, there was nothing left but for him to roll with it.

Just to make himself a more tempting target, Clint had already dropped the Colt back into its holster and his hands were balled up into fists. He shouted something to draw even more attention to himself, but Clint didn't even really know what he'd said.

All three men inside that room looked at Clint as though he'd just busted up through the floor in a burst of hellfire. Their eyes were wide for a moment and their jaws dropped open.

That reaction lasted for less than a second before they decided to unleash some hell of their own.

One of the worst mistakes any gunfighter could make was in being too full of himself. Confidence was never a bad thing, but over-confidence was never good.

Clint thought about that as he committed that all-too-popular sin and let the three men inside that shop get the drop on him. Since he'd had all of two or three seconds

to come up with his plan, Clint would have been the first
to admit that it wasn't exactly perfect. In those two or
three seconds, he figured the easiest way to get a look at
all of those men was to have them face him to take a shot.

Hopefully, in the time it took for them to aim and fire,
Clint would have been able to pick out which one among
them was not one of the killers who'd ambushed that shop
for the second time in a row. Clint watched all three of
them as everything around him seemed to slow down a
couple paces.

As those pistols swung around toward him, Clint felt
as though he was watching the scene unfold from somewhere outside of himself. There was no sound except for
the rush of his own blood. There was no scent or touch.
There was only what he could see and think.

What Clint saw was a star pinned to the shirt of the
man on the far right of the group. The badge had nearly
been lost underneath the other man's jacket, but Clint
could pick it out once the deputy turned to get a look at
him.

The deputy was holding a gun, however, and was every
bit as surprised as the other two. That meant that all three
of them swiveled and took aim at Clint, who was the
newest threat to present itself.

A look of recognition lit up the faces of the other two
and one of them squeezed off a shot before he'd even
gotten his pistol pointed in the right direction.

Clint saw the smoke erupt from that gun, but the sound
of it hardly even registered. It was no use worrying about
that bullet since it was already flying through the air, so
he put it out of his mind and prayed that the shooter
wasn't the luckiest man on earth.

Now that he had his targets in mind, Clint let his instincts run their course and felt his hand immediately drop
to the gun at his side. As soon as he'd thought about
drawing the modified Colt, the gun was in his hand and
coming out of the holster.

As soon as the gun cleared leather, it was twisted upward and aimed. Holding the gun somewhere between hip and chest level, Clint let out a single breath and pulled his trigger. The gun bucked once against his palm and then Clint was already moving it to the next target.

After spitting out two more rounds, Clint had released the last of that single breath. When he inhaled again, the world picked up its normal speed and all of his senses came back to him in a rush.

The stink of gunpowder stung his nose and his ears were vibrating with the roar of gunfire. The next thing he heard were three thumps as each of the other men dropped to the floor.

Clint was already in the process of emptying the Colt's cylinder and reloading using rounds taken from his gun belt. Rather than duck for cover, he stood his ground, filling up the broken doorway and glancing around to see if there was anyone he'd missed.

The Colt snapped shut and was dropped into Clint's holster as he started walking across the room. The only sound that could be heard was the frantic breathing of the only man besides Clint that still had a pulse.

"Jesus Christ," the deputy wheezed. The gun was still in his hand, but it was trembling like a leaf at the end of a branch being rattled in the wind. The young man's eyes darted back and forth between the other two who he'd just been talking to.

Both of the gunmen were laying spread out on the floor, their eyes stuck open and their skulls broken by one bullet hole apiece.

THIRTY-SIX

"H . . . holy . . . Jesus Christ!"

"All right," Clint said as he stepped over to the deputy and offered his hand. "Save the rest of that for church. We don't have the time right now."

Looking up at Clint, the deputy started to lift his gun, but then lowered it. Instead, he held up his empty hand and accepted Clint's help in getting to his feet. "But . . . you shot me."

Clint pulled the deputy up and gently pushed away the gun which had come dangerously close to being pointed at him. "I shot at you. There's a big difference. I just wanted to get you to drop, that's all. Are you all right?"

Patting his hand over his chest and stomach, the deputy said, "Yeah. I guess I'm fine. Who the hell are you?"

"I'm Clint Adams, a friend of Peter Banks. There's one more of those men around here. Do you know where he is?"

"Josh was out front. Is he shot?"

Clint could see the deputy was still rattled, but slowly coming out of it. "The other deputy is out there and he's fine. How many more of these men are in here?"

Hearing the sharp tone in Clint's voice was enough to shake some more of the smoke out of the deputy's head. He blinked a few more times and straightened up as

141

though he was just coming to after passing out. "I just saw these two when they pulled their guns on me." Looking over to the dead man closest to the door to the workshop, he added, "I did hear that one shouting to someone in the next room."

Clint moved like a cat as he stepped over the two bodies and headed for the workshop. The door between the two rooms was halfway open which allowed Clint to see most of what was in there.

From what he could see, the workshop was empty. There was light spilling in from the back of the room since the rear door was still open as well. When Clint pushed the door to the workshop open, he almost forgot about the bench which was still lying partially in the way. The edge and bottom of the door were both severely battered after all the pushing and shoving it had taken to get it open.

All Clint had to do was push the door with his fingertip to get it moving. It swung a little over three-quarters of the way in before knocking against the bench which was lying on its side. When he stepped sideways into the room, Clint drew the Colt in a smooth, single motion, bringing the pistol up to bear on anyone who might be waiting for him inside the workshop. He spun around to check out one section of the room and then hopped over the bench so he could look behind the door.

Each time, he found nothing.

Clint relaxed just a little bit as he made his way to the back of the room, looking in every nook and cranny in the process. He got to the back door without coming across another soul and then stepped outside to get a look at the back lot.

It seemed especially quiet outside. The flakes of snow drifting through the air seemed to absorb every bit of sound, giving the day that special quiet that was reserved only for the winter. Clint's steps sounded especially loud in contrast to the outside calm. He could even hear some voices and activity coming from the nearby streets.

Since they hadn't found anything else of interest, Clint's eyes followed some of the falling snow as it twisted and turned on its way to the ground. When the flakes met the frosted dirt, Clint spotted something else that put a triumphant smile on his face.

Just then, something else broke the silence, but it was a sound familiar enough to keep Clint from reacting out of turn. The breathing was just as haggard as when he'd last heard it coming from the first deputy's mouth and the younger man's steps had been loud enough to announce his presence way ahead of time.

"There you are," the deputy said. "I waited outside as long as I could, but then I heard the shots. I came in to see if I could help, but you were already gone, so I came back around and—"

"Josh," Clint said. "That's your name, right?"

The deputy nodded. "Yes, sir."

"Good. Shut up, Josh. You did fine. Did you catch up with your friend?"

"Yeah. Will told me what you did and—"

All Clint had to do this time was raise his hand and the deputy stopped talking. So far, Clint hadn't taken his eyes off the ground. Lifting one finger on that raised hand, he slowly twisted his hand and pointed down, leading the deputy's eyes to the same spot near his boots. When the deputy saw what Clint had been looking at, he smiled a bit as well.

Footprints.

If there was a worst possible time to try and make a clean getaway, it was in freshly fallen snow. Even the prints Clint and Peter had left on their way into the workshop were almost completely filled in. That left a few fresher ones left by the men who'd kicked in the back door as well as an even fresher set on top of those.

"You see those?" Clint asked.

"I sure do."

"I'm following those as far as they'll take me before

this snow gets any worse. You and Will go tell the sheriff
what went on here."

"I uh . . . can't just let you go," the deputy said in a
wavering voice. "There's dead men here and you need to
come with me to see the sheriff."

Clint was already starting to walk along the trail of
footprints left behind by the last person to come through
that back door. "I'm not leaving town, kid. I'll check in
as soon as I can."

"But that's not the way I'm supposed—"

"Let him go," came another voice from inside the workshop. It was Will and he nodded once Josh turned to look
at him. "He saved my life. I think that counts for something."

Looking over his shoulder, Clint saw both of the deputies looking back at him. They motioned for him to get
moving and headed back into the workshop.

THIRTY-SEVEN

As nice as it would have been to have those tracks in the snow lead directly to the man who'd left them, Clint didn't expect for one moment that it was going to play out that way. Instead, they led down the alley and out the other side before turning off onto the main street. From there, the tracks became just one set among dozens that had overrun it in the last minute or two.

People walked by on the street, tramping all over the footprints along the way. There were plenty more right behind them, not to mention the horses and wagons that were rolling over the tracks as well. Once Clint saw the tracks disappear amid so many others, he looked around one last time, hoping to see something that might point him in the right direction.

The snow was still falling, but this time it didn't lead his eyes in any particular way. There was nobody running for cover or waving a gun. There wasn't even anyone shoving someone else aside in their haste to get where they were going. The trail had gone colder than the tips of Clint's freezing toes, but that didn't mean the pursuit was worthless.

For one thing, whoever had left those tracks had been in an awful hurry to get away. That told Clint that the attack was over for the moment. Also, he'd only spotted

one set of tracks leading away from the gun shop. That
told him that there was only one man who'd made it away
from there in one piece.

In his mind, Clint checked off three more of Major
Waterman's men. That left about four more he had to
worry about and one of those was injured. The odds
hadn't been too good when this all started, but at least
they were beginning to shape up somewhat.

Suddenly, Clint wondered what the Major was doing at
that moment. Was the older man waiting to hear a report
from his killers, or was he still sitting at his card table
waiting to finish the game? The answer to that would have
to wait just a little while. Clint had another more important appointment to keep.

Having walked the last block with his eyes pointed toward
the ground, Clint needed to take a moment to get his bear-
ings. Fortunately, he'd wound up heading in the direction
of the Gemmell Lodge. Unfortunately, that also meant the
man he'd been following was headed that way as well.
Clint could only hope that was a coincidence and hurry
up to meet with Peter.

Along the way, he heard plenty of talk about the gunshots that had rocked the small town not too long ago.
Everyone was too wrapped up in their gossip, however,
to take much notice as Clint slipped right by them. After
passing the front of the restaurant, Clint circled around
the block and ducked between two buildings on the opposite side.

Being behind a restaurant, the alley was much more of
an assault against his sense of smell than the one next to
Peter's place. There were crates piled up along the dark
passage and some of which were filled with rotten foods
of all kinds. Some of it was meat and some was fruit and
vegetables. The only thing it all had in common was that
it smelled bad.

It smelled very, very bad.

Clint pulled his bandana up over his mouth and nose

as he passed by a large outhouse, knowing the stench would only get that much worse. As soon as he walked by the smaller shack, Clint caught a bit of movement coming from that direction. He looked over to tip his hat to whoever was on their way out of the toilet and found himself staring down the barrel of a gun.

Actually, he found himself staring down half a dozen barrels.

"For the love of god, Peter, will you put that gun down?" Clint said in a voice muffled by the bandana. "Hasn't it gotten you into enough trouble already?"

Once Clint pulled the bandana back down around his neck, Peter let out a deep, relieved breath.

"My apologies, Clint. I thought you were one of them."

"Isn't there someplace better we can talk instead of behind this shithouse?"

"I didn't want to go inside with this contraption attached to my arm," Peter explained. "But I didn't want to take the gun off until you arrived, either."

"Well now that I'm here, let's get inside."

Peter was only too happy to meet Clint's request. He got the crank-gun off of his arm with a few quick adjustments. Once the metal band was loose, Peter dropped the gun into the inner pocket of his coat. Although the weapon created a hell of a bulge under the Englishman's left arm, at least it was out of sight.

"Come on," Peter said as he walked toward the door which was marked NOT AN ENTRANCE. "We can slip in through the kitchen."

Peter knocked on the door and waited. There was a lot of noise coming from inside, so he knocked again a little harder. Soon, the door came open a crack and a face peeked out.

"Try the next door over, buddy," came a gruff man's voice. "If it's locked, head around front."

"It's Peter Banks. I need to get in this way."

The man who'd just been shouting out through the slender opening now stuck his head all the way out so he could see who it was that had knocked, Clint recognized the face as one of the many that had come out to greet him when he and Peter had enjoyed their free breakfast earlier in the day.

"Peter! Are you all right?" the man in the kitchen asked. "I heard there was shooting at your place."

"I'm fine. Right now, my friend and I need someplace to rest for a bit without being seen. Do you think we could trouble you to stay here a bit?"

"No trouble at all. Come on in."

Clint followed Peter through the door and into a kitchen bustling with activity. From there, they were taken to another smaller room packed with crates that gave off an odor vaguely resembling the one in the alley. It wasn't quite as bad since the food there wasn't all spoiled, but it was nearly as overpowering.

Then again, it beat the hell out of freezing behind an outhouse.

THIRTY-EIGHT

Late afternoon was passing into early evening. The sky was darkening and already the air had taken on even more of a cold bite. Winds howled down the street and people rushed to wherever they needed to go with their coats pulled tightly around them and their faces covered by scarves and upturned collars.

Watching all of this through the window of the Double Diamond, Major Waterman lifted a glass of whiskey to his lips and tipped it back. The brown liquid slid down his throat, heating up his insides as it worked its way down.

Like most of the town, he'd heard the chatter of the crank-gun when Peter had fired it behind his shop. The sound was barely audible through the plate glass of the window, but since the Major had been straining his ears for the sound of gunfire, he'd managed to recognize it when it came.

More gunshots followed, causing him to smirk grimly as he watched the people outside his window rush back and forth, trying to figure out what was going on.

Since then, he'd been waiting.

Waiting to see his men come back from their appointed errand.

149

Waiting to hear news about the fatalities at the Eng lishman's gun shop.

Waiting to feel the weight of that deadly contraption Banks had created in his own two hands.

As time went by, Major Waterman was just waiting to see if his men were going to come back at all. Once they did, they wouldn't have to wait too long to hear just how much the Major hated waiting.

Finally, the Major turned away from the window and headed back to the table where Marland and Bill were still playing with a couple newer arrivals that had descended upon the empty seats like vultures. Reaching out, Waterman took hold of Bill's shoulder and all but dragged the younger man to his feet.

"I want you to get off your ass," Waterman snarled. "Get down to that goddamn limey's shop and see what the hell is taking those other two so fucking long."

The younger man with the scars on his face fought back the profanities that came reflexively to his mind at being manhandled in such a way. If it was any other person on the face of the earth besides the Major at the other end of that arm, Bill would surely have sent him to his grave. As it was, he twisted out of the Major's grasp and straightened his clothes with a few annoyed tugs.

"All right," Bill said. "I'll go right now."

"Goddamn right you will. And don't come back here until you either find those two or their bodies. Understand me?"

Bill grumbled that he understood just fine and stormed toward the front door. Grabbing his hat and coat from the rack as he went, the young man threw himself into the garments and headed outside.

Waterman's eyes were burning through the kid's back the entire time. Only after Bill could no longer even be seen through the front window did the Major turn his attention back to the card game he'd interrupted.

"Marland," Waterman said in a voice that was calmer, but not by much. "Come here for a moment."

The portly man got up from his chair, wheezing as though it took all of his strength to complete the task. Finally, he was on his feet and waddling after the Major as the other man stepped up to the bar.

"Having Banks's friend in town is playing hell with our plans," Major Waterman said after downing the rest of his whiskey. "And if things don't go right for me, they don't go right for anyone else down the line."

"You know who Clint Adams is, right?" Marland asked.

"Yes, I do. Should I just pack up and write this off as a loss just because some gunfighter breezes into town?"

"Some folks might consider that option when they find out that the gunfighter is Clint Adams."

Waterman set his jaw and looked squarely into the other man's eyes. His fists were clenched so tightly that his knuckles were turning white under the pressure. "If you think I'm not up to this, just say so. If you want to step up and see how much better you could do, feel free, Marland."

The portly man shook his head and waved away Waterman's menacing words with the back of his hand. "No, not at all, Major. This is your show. I wouldn't dream of taking it away from you."

"Good. See that you keep that in mind." With that, Major Waterman let his fists uncurl and allowed his shoulders to relax slightly. He turned his back on the portly figure and headed back to the window where he could once again take up his vigil.

Marland ordered the barkeep to top off his drink and started walking back to the table that had been his home for the better part of the last several days. Before reaching his own chair, he stopped off at another section of the bar where a man in a dark jacket was waiting.

"How many did you bring for this?" Marland asked, without looking in the other man's direction.

The dark figure didn't bother turning around when he

replied, "I brought more than enough with me, but I've already lost more than I like."

"How many is that?"

"Two."

"The Major's already lost more than that."

"That's because the Major is a small-time card cheat with over-eager punks working for him. My men were good men. One of them is worth five of those others."

Checking his watch to make him look busy, Marland flipped open the timepiece and gazed down at its face. He spoke as though he was grumbling to himself rather than the man standing at the bar. "Then you better not lose any more. Clint Adams is part of this now, but the goal is the same. We need to get that weapon no matter what."

"And what if your friend the Major somehow gets his paws on it first? The only way to get it from him would be to wrangle it out of his dead hands. What about that?"

Snapping the watch shut and stuffing it back into his pocket, Marland rasped, "No matter what."

THIRTY-NINE

The owners of the restaurant brought Clint and Peter another free meal, which went a long way to combat the overpowering smell of the storage closet they were using as a hiding spot. Neither man had much of an appetite, but Clint ate what he could knowing that he would need all the strength he could get.

Peter shook his head, poked at the food on his tin plate and didn't eat a bite. "This is a bloody awful mess, isn't it?"

"I don't know," Clint said. "I've seen worse." He stopped and rubbed his chin for a moment. "Not a lot worse, actually, but I've seen some pretty bad ones anyway."

That got Peter to smile a little, but the moment quickly passed. "What the blazes was I thinking, Clint? How could I be so stupid?"

"You're not stupid. You're just . . . focused. You've been doing this work for a long time for a lot of people. How were you supposed to know which ones would turn out this way?"

"I was supposed to know, damn it. That's part of being responsible and in this line of work a man must be responsible." Peter lifted the plate to his mouth as though he was about to take a bite, but then threw it across the room in a burst of motion. "I just need to get out of this town. Once I'm gone, this will just have to pass. If it doesn't, at least I won't be here to spark any more gun battles. Either way, at least you won't have to put yourself at risk on my account."

Clint took a moment to eat a few more bites of what was on his plate. Since he was only going through the motions to fill his belly, he didn't even really notice what exactly he'd been served. Once he could tell that Peter had calmed himself a little bit, Clint said, "It doesn't matter where you go. If those men are connected to the military, they'll want that gun. Even if they're not with the army, they'll still want it and they'll find you wherever you go."

"I hope this isn't supposed to be making me feel better."

"It isn't. It's meant as a wake-up call, Peter. The truth is you should have been more responsible. But now that the mess has started, you need to help clean it up. The first thing you need to do is admit you're in over your head."

The Englishman looked over at Clint and shrugged. "If I did that, I would never have been able to make this crank-gun in the first place." Before Clint could respond, Peter nodded and said, "I know what you're saying, though. Perhaps I can manage to stay in here for a bit and keep out of trouble until things die down a touch."

"That's close to what I had in mind, but not completely. We definitely need to fix this situation, but it needs to be done quickly and cleanly. The best way to do all of that just might be to use the best trump card in this particular deck."

Peter's eyes naturally drifted down to the bulky weapon that was still tucked away inside his coat. "I can show you how to use this, although I can't say I'm happy about resorting to such extreme—"

"That's not quite what I had in mind," Clint interrupted. "At least, not as anything but a last resort."

The Englishman seemed relieved, but only for a moment. "What, then?"

"You do need to stay out of sight, but only for a little bit. Do you think you'll be safe in this place for a while longer?"

Peter nodded immediately. "I've known the owners of this establishment ever since I moved to this town. If I can't trust them, then I can't trust anyone in Gemmell."

"That's good enough for me. You stay here until I come back for you. In the meantime, I need you to make some special modifications to that gun. Do you need me to bring back any tools from your shop?"

"That depends on what you want me to do."

Clint went over his basic thoughts for the crank-gun with its creator. Even though he was unfamiliar with that particular weapon, Clint's own gunsmithing skills were good enough for him to make some suggestions on the quickest way to get the job done.

When Clint was finished, Peter couldn't help but grin proudly. "I see you've been practicing our trade in the years since I last saw you."

"You'd be amazed how much practice I've had since then. There's something else I need you to work on while you're here."

It didn't take long for Clint to describe his second project. As he did, the Englishman nodded and even stopped him before he went into too much detail.

"That's all you need to say," Peter said, cutting in on Clint's description. "I've actually put something like that together for another client of mine who did some bounty hunting in Mexico."

"So you can make that for me as well?"

"No problem."

"And what about the tools?" Clint asked. "How much do you need from your shop?"

Shrugging, Peter glanced around the storage room and thought for a second. "You shouldn't have to go back there at all. First off, it's much too dangerous. And secondly, both of these jobs are fairly simple matters. It should only require basic tools which I should be able to find right around here. The owners shouldn't have any trouble getting what I need."

"Are you sure?"

"Definitely."

"Great," Clint said. "That part's settled, then. The rest is up to me."

"And what might that entail?"

"My first thought was to get a better idea of what I'm going up against. I've met the Major and got a good feel for what he's dealing with. If I'm right, he doesn't exactly have an army behind him and should be running low on men to back him up."

Furrowing his brow, Peter shook his head. "I don't think he's the one behind all of this. My contact from the military only shows up to pick up the orders once they're done. Other than that, I get orders from runners and telegrams."

"He may be called the Major, but I doubt that's any type of genuine rank," Clint pointed out. "If anything, he's someone that got wind of what you were doing and decided to snatch it up for himself. That crank-gun is worth an awful lot to the right people."

"And it's worth even more to the wrong ones," Peter said, finishing Clint's thought. "I may be naive, but I've been around long enough to know that."

"Hopefully, this Major is our main concern, but something tells me there's more to it than that. I need to find out if there's another player in town or if the Major is the highest roller."

Shaking his head, Peter said, "You've been spending too much time at those gambling parlors. I told you those would get the better of you."

Clint ignored the parental tone in Peter's voice and moved ahead with his own train of thought. "I need to get closer to the Major because he's the next link in this chain. If there is someone else after that gun, then my bet is he'll know about it. Men like that make it their business to know those things."

"So you'll be meeting with the Major again, I presume?"

"There's not enough time to get the information that way. I'll have to take the next best route." Clint stood up and headed for the door.

"And which route might that be?" Peter asked.

"If I can't get any closer to the Major, I'll just have to talk to someone who can . . . or already has."

FORTY

Marvin was still behind the bar at the Double Diamond when the sun finally sank beneath the horizon. Although the night was arriving earlier then than at any other time of year, it felt as though the dusk had been approaching all day long. Now that most of the daylight was officially gone, there were more people than ever inside the gambling club.

Filling a row of mugs from the tap, Marvin turned around and was just in time to see his favorite sight within the entire place. "Good lord almighty!" he said. "You look sweeter than candy in that dress, Amanda."

The blonde turned to toss a glance over her shoulder. "And looking is all you better do, Marvin."

Both of them got disapproving stares from the serious gamblers that didn't go away until both the barkeep and the waitress shut their mouths. Amanda dropped off her drinks and went back to lean against the bar.

"There's something in that walk of yours," Marvin said, "When will I be able to get my hands on you for myself?"

"I do feel good tonight. If you were here earlier, you'd know why."

"I was here earlier and I do know why. I just wish it was me you took upstairs."

"If I thought you could make me holler like that, I just

might do that someday." She enjoyed watching Marvin's jaw drop as she leaned over the bar and arched her back in the way that caught every man's attention. "Maybe you can prove yourself to me, big man."

"Yeah. If I ever thought you were serious, I might just do that someday."

They held their eyes on each other for a moment before both of their faces cracked into smiles. Marvin wasn't the type to flirt so shamelessly, but that had just become the normal way he and Amanda talked to each other. All the real sexual tension had gone out of it. Well, for her anyway.

Suddenly, Marvin's eyes were drawn toward the front door. When he saw the tall, imposing figure that came through it, he lost all of the playfulness that Amanda had brought out of him. He reflexively backed off a step when he saw that figure was heading straight for him.

Amanda looked over to see what had drained the color from Marvin's face and quickly found the figure for herself. It was a man with broad shoulders covered in a long duster. The collar of the coat was pulled up and a dark scarf was wrapped around his neck, both of which all but covered most of his face. The only part of him that she could really make out was the upper curve of his nose and the sliver of his eyes peering out from beneath his hat.

Everyone else inside the club glanced up for a second. Once they saw the man wasn't headed straight for one of the games, they turned their attention back to what they were doing. The Major was sitting at his game and took a hard look at the stranger as well. But the figure seemed more interested in getting a drink and Waterman had more important things on his mind.

"What can I get for you?" Marvin asked, unable to keep the nervousness from his voice.

Amanda knew better than to keep her eyes trained on the figure now that he was close enough to smell the perfume she wore. Having spent most of her time around

gamblers and card cheats, she knew when to strut and
when to quietly walk away. This was the time for the
latter and she calmly turned her back on the figure, hunch-
ing her shoulders just enough to cover a bit of her plung-
ing neckline.

Suddenly, the stranger's hand shot out to close around
Amanda's elbow. His grip wasn't tight enough to hurt her,
but it was strong enough to keep her from taking another
step.

"I want a word with the lady," the stranger said.

Marvin stepped up to the bar, noticing that the dark
figure had caught the attention of Marland as well as Bill
who was just now starting to walk over.

"Look mister," Marvin said. "I can get you a drink and
she can even serve it to you. Just don't start any trouble.
There's been enough of that around here already."

"Brave talk from a barkeep," the stranger said. With his
free hand, the man pushed up the tip of his hat and lifted
his chin to reveal some of the face hidden behind his scarf.
"I didn't think you had it in you, Marvin."

The barkeep's eyes widened and he almost spoke loud
enough to alert the whole room. Before he did, he was
stopped by the figure who now placed his finger over his
lips to shush him. Keeping his voice down to a whisper,
Marvin said, "Mister Adams? Is that really you?"

When she heard that, Amanda twisted around to get a
better look at him. A smile flashed over her face for a
split second, but then she moved to step around Clint's
back so she was between him and Bill, who was almost
close enough to hear what was going on.

"You almost had me fooled, Carl," she said, slapping
Clint's shoulder. Looking up at Bill, she asked, "Is there
something wrong?"

"I was just about to ask you the same thing," Bill replied.

Amanda laughed and let out a breath. "Carl here just
gave me a fright, is all." Her eyes darted toward the back
of the room. "Jesus, what's the Major pissed at now?"

Bill hadn't stepped back and was still glaring at the back of Clint's head, right up until Amanda mentioned Major Waterman. Then, he rolled his eyes and turned around to see Waterman staring directly at him. "Shit, you're right. I better go see what he wants." Bill shot one more glance in Clint's direction, but was quickly diverted by Amanda's beaming smile. "Let me know if this one gives you any trouble."

With that, Bill stomped away and headed toward the Major's table.

Marvin let out a slow whistle. "That was close. You think he saw anything?"

"If he did, I'm sure we'd know about it," Amanda replied. She took hold of Clint's hand and led him toward the front door. "Come on. Let's go somewhere we can talk."

FORTY-ONE

Amanda dragged Clint out of the Double Diamond and round the building on the opposite side of where the narrower structure was. By the time she pulled him away from the street and tightly up against her, she was fighting to control her laughter.

Even though he hadn't been in the laughing mood himself, Clint couldn't help but feel his lips forming a smile. "Is there something funny that I missed here?" he asked.

"No, no. I'm just so happy to see you. With all the shooting and the way the Major's been talking, it sounded as though you were as good as dead." Her arms locked around Clint's neck and she squeezed him with all her strength. "I'm so glad to see you again. I truly am."

It felt good when Clint wrapped his arms around her and Amanda's body fitted that much more against his own. "I know. It's good for me too."

Now that the sun was long gone, the wind felt that much colder as it whipped down the street and between every last building. Although Clint had been feeling the chill all the way down into the marrow of his bones, it was affecting him less the more he held Amanda in his arms. She nuzzled her face against his neck, kissing him gently after peeling back the coat collar and scarf with her teeth.

"I knew if anyone could make the Major eat his words, it would be you," she said in between kisses. "I heard him talking about how he was going to make the Gunsmith look the fool right before having him shot."

"You heard that, huh?"

She nodded. The movement of her head made her lips press against him a little harder and her fragrant blonde hair brush across his face. "I heard him say that and I tried not to spit in the bastard's face."

"Actually, that's sort of why I came to find you."

After one last squeeze, she looked up into his eyes and asked, "You came to find me to hear me babble on like this?"

"No. I came because I know you must hear an awful lot that Major Waterman says. Not just now or since I've gotten here, but all the time. I've seen the way he looks at you. He must want to impress you with some of his big plans or money-making deals."

She'd seemed confused at first, but now Amanda nodded slowly and her grin turned from happy to sly. "You think I'm your own personal spy. Is that it?"

Clint returned her smile again as he felt her hands move beneath his coat. "Something like that. Is there something wrong with being my personal spy?"

"I can tell you one thing you'd find pretty interesting."

"Yeah? What is it?"

"Oh no," Amanda replied. Keeping a firm grip on Clint's belt, she twisted herself around so that when she turned further into the shadows, Clint came right along with her. "I may be a spy, but I don't work for free."

Clint was standing in front of Amanda and they were both in the thick, dark shadows just beyond the boardwalk alongside the Double Diamond Club. Her back was against the wall and she was almost completely hidden by Clint's open coat. When he leaned in to kiss her deeply on the lips, his hat covered most of her face.

She tasted sweet as ever and Clint wasn't in any hurry for the kiss to end. His tongue slipped into her mouth,

164   J. R. ROBERTS

which made her squirm against him. Amanda's arms slid
deeper inside his coat, tugging at his shirt and waistband
until she could feel his bare skin against her fingers.

The kiss ended eventually and Clint only moved his
head back enough so he could speak. "There are benefits
to being my personal spy, you know."

Grinning, Amanda took a quick, playful bite on Clint's
lower lip. "If you think that's all the payment I'm after,
you're sorely mistaken."

Before Clint could say anything else, he felt Amanda's
hand slide between his legs. She massaged him until his
penis was almost fully erect. "That man you were playing
poker with . . . Marland . . . he's not just some fat card
player."

"Really? Tell me more."

"He doesn't say much to anyone except to the Major
when they think nobody else is around. He didn't even
say much in front of me, but the Major likes having me
around."

"And I wonder why that is."

Amanda's hand was still stroking him as she moved in
to kiss him passionately on the mouth. As she did, she
also managed to unbutton Clint's pants and slide her hand
down inside them. "Because he hopes that I'll do something like this to him."

Trying to keep his mind on business was a difficult
proposition just then. All Clint wanted to do was feel his
naked body against Amanda's. Her tight curves and lithe
muscles writhed against him, teasing him even through
the clothes they were both wearing. With that in mind,
Clint moved his hands lower along her hips, sliding down
over her buttocks and back up to her waist.

"At least you didn't lie about one thing," he said. "You
didn't put your underwear back on."

She looked at him hungrily, her eyes narrowing slightly
when she felt his hands upon her body.

"What did you hear Marland say?" Clint whispered.

"That he had some men waiting in another hotel here

in town. The Major kept asking how good they were with
guns and if they were good enough to take down a man
like you." She pulled in a quick breath as Clint began
pulling up her skirt and bunching it around her waist.
"Marland told him that his men could kill anyone so long
as they were paid enough."

"And Major Waterman is willing to pay them?"

"He already has. The money that he loses to Marland
in the poker games is his way of making the payment
without anyone else knowing."

"And you heard all of this?"

"All of that and more," she said softly. "But like I told
you before, it's not free."

Clint's hands were underneath her skirt and grazing
along the soft, bare skin of her thigh. He could feel her
tensing slightly in the cold, but he moved in close enough
to shield her from most of it. People would walk by occasionally on the boardwalk, but their eyes were focused
on the Double Diamond and they were moving quickly
past to get into the warmth of its walls.

Besides that, it would have taken a bat to see into the
thick darkness that covered Clint and Amanda like an inky
shroud.

His fingers already warmed by Amanda's skin, Clint
slid them between her legs until he could feel the downy
thatch of hair. She grabbed hold of him even tighter and
moaned softly when his fingers slid through that soft hair
and along the moist lips between her legs.

"The Major needs to get ahold of that gun before to-
morrow, or he loses some kind of finder's fee. He made
promises and is supposed to deliver the gun in a few days.
Marland is using the Major's boys as a way to get close
enough to the gun to take it."

"Why hasn't he just taken it already?" Clint asked.

"Because he only got into town the night before you
did."

"How many men does Marland have with him?"

"I don't know. He never said. I did hear him say that

there was going to be a meet at midnight tonight where they could gather all their men together and make one last play against you. They just decided this about half an hour ago. Marland was so wrapped up in the idea that he didn't even notice me standing there."

"What about the Major? Did he see you?"

"He saw. He just didn't want me to leave."

Clint's fingers slid inside of her and his other hand moved over her bare buttocks. "I know exactly how he feels."

FORTY-TWO

Clint was awfully glad there was still a ways to go before midnight. Even if bullets started to fly around his head at that very moment, he doubted he'd be able to pull himself away from Amanda's warm, writhing body. More than that, he doubted he'd even want to.

Her trim frame fit within his coat to the point where she was almost swallowed up by it. She slid her foot up along the back of Clint's leg, grinding her hips against him as she tugged his pants down further. Leaning her head back, Amanda let out a slow breath as Clint continued to massage her pussy. Wisps of steam curled out of her mouth as she savored the feel of him inside of her.

Clint's penis was rock hard as Amanda's hand continued to stroke up and down along its length. Feeling his hands slide beneath her clothes made his heart beat faster. Feeling her pussy become more and more wet around his fingers made him almost desperate to give in to every animal instinct that raged inside of him.

His heart beat even faster within his chest when he felt Amanda's hands pulling his pants down just low enough to free him from them. One of her arms and legs were curled all the way around him, tucked up underneath his coat so that the one piece of clothing could cover them both.

Clint moved his hand between her legs, sliding his finger out of her and tracing a smooth line along her soft inner thigh. From there, he kept moving back until he could reach behind her with both hands and cup her firm, rounded buttocks.

The moment Amanda felt where his hands were, she hopped up so she could wrap her other leg around him. She clasped her hands together behind his neck and pulled herself up as he lifted her off her feet. It took a bit of adjusting, but soon their bodies were fitted perfectly together; her back against the wall and Clint pressing against her front.

Climbing over him as though she no longer feared gravity, Amanda opened her legs wide until she felt the tip of his cock slip inside of her. They both let out a satisfied gasp as she shifted her hips until she'd managed to work half of his length into herself.

With a slow, forward thrust, Clint pushed all the way inside, burying his cock as deep as it would go and pushing her harder against the wall. He could feel her fingers digging into the flesh of his neck and shoulders and could hear her moaning softy into his ear.

Holding her in both hands, Clint could feel Amanda's body straining every time he thrust into her. Whenever he slid out, she used her heels and legs to pull him close again, pushing her own hips forward while spreading her knees as though she couldn't wait to feel him drive inside of her one more time.

Her body was hot and writhing, accepting him within herself and groaning with pleasure every time he buried his cock between her legs. It wasn't long before they had built up some power with their efforts and a rhythm which took them both to new heights in pleasure.

Loosening her grip around his neck slightly, Amanda opened her eyes and stared into Clint's, grinning lewdly as she tightened her legs around his waist. She looked away for a second, glancing over toward the boardwalk where a small group of figures was walking by and noisily talking about where they were headed.

Clint couldn't tell exactly what those people were saying. The blood was still rushing too swiftly through his head for that. He could hear their footsteps clomping over the boardwalk, though. They were already close and getting closer with every second.

When he could see them through the opening between the buildings, Clint thought for sure that he and Amanda would be spotted in the middle of what they were doing. Amanda probably thought that as well, but her reaction to it was grinding her hips slowly against him, moving him in and out of her as though she was trying desperately to make him break the silence.

For a second, Clint thought he was going to do just that. Although being discovered by those random folks wouldn't have done much besides embarrass him, he still wasn't chomping at the bit to be found that way. When Amanda started moving that certain way, slipping the lips of her vagina up and down his shaft in a slow massage, he thought that he would have no choice but to throw himself back into the fit of lovemaking no matter who was watching.

Those people kept walking and only one of them glanced over in the couple's direction. Between the shadows of the night and Clint's dark overcoat, he and Amanda were practically invisible to the casual eye. Since that was the case, those folks kept right on walking and talking, oblivious to what they'd almost seen.

Clint looked back to Amanda and was about to tease her in a scolding manner, but was stopped by the look on her face. She was still staring at him and her eyes were burning into his as she concentrated on what she was doing. The smile on her mouth was tight and the tip of her tongue darted out to moisten her lips.

She was still moving her hips, but now she was putting even more effort into it, grinding back and forth, shifting her weight so his hardness rubbed up against her in the best possible way. It didn't matter that she was the one being carried. Amanda rode him as though Clint was the one on his back and she was the lover in control.

Clint had never felt such intense sensation. Between the cold air and snow swirling around them, the possibility that they might be found making love in the open, and the passionate way that Amanda used every muscle in her body to pleasure them both, Clint thought he might explode with the ecstasy that surged through him. Connected to him in more ways than one at that moment, Amanda was feeling the same thing.

Once again, she clenched her eyes shut and pressed her head back against the wall. She was pumping her hips as if desperate to feel him and Clint was thrusting in and out of her as well. Between the two of them, they built up enough heat so that the winter night was all but forgotten.

There was no snow and nobody else to find them. There was just Clint and Amanda, each of them pushing the other to the height of passion until the inevitable explosion finally came. Amanda's eyes shot open and she pulled in a powerful breath.

Clint thought for sure she was going to let out a scream that would wake up the entire town, but instead she leaned in and buried her face in his shoulder where his coat opened to reveal the shirt beneath. She screamed into the clothing as her entire body trembled.

That was more than enough to push Clint over the edge as well and he pumped into her one last time as his climax all but overtook him.

Even after the waves of pleasure subsided, he held her there for a little while longer. Finally, Amanda lowered her legs and allowed Clint to set her down upon her own feet. She straightened herself up a little bit as Clint pulled his own clothes back on.

He started to take a step back just to give her some space, but Amanda grabbed hold of his arm and nearly pulled him off his feet.

"Don't you go anywhere," she said. "I need to

straighten up a little first. We are still in the open and everything, you know."

"Now you're getting bashful?" Clint asked with a laugh.

"Just stand there for one more second."

She pulled her top up so that she wasn't about to fall out of it and then tugged her skirt down over her waist. Clint watched the way she moved when she did that, shifting her hips slightly and straightening her dress until she looked pretty close to how she had before they'd ducked into the shadows.

"Will I see you after midnight?" she asked.

"Definitely. Maybe not right away, but I'm not going to forget you anytime soon. Just be sure to keep safe if anything does happen. And if anyone ever asks, you never said more than two words to me."

She nodded and gave him another kiss. "Take care, Clint Adams. I'll be here whenever you decide to come back."

FORTY-THREE

Eleven o'clock.

Clint left Amanda so she could get back to work and act as though nothing had happened. Although he knew better than to think he'd be able to stay much longer in Gemmell, he had every intention of making sure she was alright before he left. That was something he vowed to do once everything else was wrapped up. Until that time, however, there was still plenty left to be done.

Sticking to the shadows and alleyways, Clint made his way back to the Gemmell Lodge where Peter was hopefully still hiding. He prayed that the Englishman hadn't gotten a burr under his saddle the way he'd done the last time Clint had left him. If Peter decided to strike out on his own yet again, Clint figured there wasn't much he could do about it.

But Peter hadn't gone anywhere in the time Clint had been away. In fact, he was in pretty much the same spot that Clint had left him. The food storage room still smelled overpoweringly of different scents and it wasn't until that second time that Clint realized why the odor hit him so hard. The storage area would have smelled that way anytime, but compared to the clean purity of the crisp winter air, the smells in that place seemed especially harsh.

Clint did his best to put those things out of his mind when he met up with Peter once again. It was good to distract himself every once in a while just to keep his feet on the ground, but the time had come to focus on nothing but the task at hand. Apparently, Peter had been thinking the same thing.

The Englishman sat huddled over his crank-gun which was in two separate pieces. Various tools were scattered about, but nothing more complex than a hammer and a pair of pliers. There was a small crowbar as well, along with some sheets of iron and some lengths of rope.

"How are the projects coming?" Clint asked.

Without looking up from what he was doing, Peter replied, "Done with one and almost with the other."

"What about that?" Clint asked, pointing toward the dismantled weapon on the floor.

"Finished. I'm keeping it open until it's time for us to . . . well . . . do whatever we're doing. That reminds me. What exactly are we doing?"

"I met with someone who is close to Major Waterman. She said that she did hear some things which turned out to be even more helpful than I'd hoped for."

Clint gave Peter a quick rundown on what Amanda had told him. Still working on his last project, the Englishman nodded every so often to show that he was listening. By the time Clint was done with his account, Peter was done with his project and he held it up for inspection.

Glancing over Peter's work, Clint began to nod as well. He looked over the finished piece and then back to its creator. "Do you think this will hold up?"

"It had bloody well better, that's all I have to say. Besides, if it doesn't I'll be the first to know."

"Yeah, but it'll be too late to fix it by then."

"Don't worry about that. You've got plenty more to worry about the way it is and most of it is my bloody fault."

"Nobody blames you, Peter. You were doing your job and someone decided to take advantage of you. It's not like you haven't done any good with all those other jobs. I hear there was an entire regiment that made it through a skirmish two years ago thanks to one of your improvements on their rifles."

"That doesn't matter," Peter said with a dismissive wave. "I botched this up and because of me the world might have to deal with this little horror I concocted. What the hell was I thinking, Clint?"

"You were thinking about doing your job. Jesus, don't start talking ethics with me or you might drag me down there with you. We do the best we can with what we've got and that's all we can ever do."

Peter reached down and fit the two pieces of the crank-gun back together. "So we have until midnight before the rest of these thugs get together and figure out a way to hunt me down?"

"That's right."

"And what do we do once that happens?"

"We save them all the trouble of hunting for us, because we'll both already be there."

Nodding, Peter put down the gun and picked up the other project he'd been working on. "Now that I think about it, perhaps this piece could still use some work."

FORTY-FOUR

Midnight.

Major Waterman pulled his coat around him and let out a slow, chattering breath. The night had only gotten colder until his breath was nearly ripped from his lungs the moment he stepped out of the Double Diamond. The word had been sent out to the rest of his men that they were to forget about the rest of their duties and meet in the empty lot behind the feed store owned by the Major himself.

That store was the first place Waterman had purchased when he'd come to Gemmell and it was fitting that he meet there on the night before he intended on putting the town behind him. Marland's men had been summoned as well, pulled away from their scattered posts all over town so they could all hear what Waterman had to say.

The Major had never seen more than three months inside a uniform and he liked the notion of so many men obeying him as though he'd truly earned his rank instead of stole it. But that was in the past and Waterman seldom ever thought about those days anymore. He'd gone under his self-appointed title for so long that even he sometimes wondered if he hadn't served in the army.

Marland, on the other hand, was the picture of a retired military man. Now that he was no longer trying to go unnoticed, he straightened his back until it hurt and he sucked in the gut that had made him look so slovenly before. He strutted through the night, ignoring the cold. Snow gathered on his shoulders and face the way it might collect upon a statue. As he stood and waited for his men to arrive, he moved just as much as any other statue would under the circumstances.

Standing next to the Major, Bill shifted on his feet and slapped his arms together to try and beat back the cold. Another man walked around the feed store to stand on Waterman's other flank, soon to be joined by a third.

"All of my men are here," Waterman said. "Right on time."

Marland looked over the three gunmen and almost smirked. "Yeah. Real punctual. All three of them."

The muscles in Major Waterman's jaw tightened and he snarled through clenched teeth. "These are all that's left after that goddamn Adams showed up. Not to mention the ones that got caught in front of that gun you want so badly."

"And what would your men have done with Adams if that gun hadn't been operational?" Marland asked. "Played a few hands of poker with him?"

"You were sitting at that same table with me, you arrogant prick. All we needed to do was keep Adams busy while my men tracked him down."

"That may have been the case, but it was my men who found and confronted him."

"They should have kept back like I wanted," Waterman shot back, jabbing his finger toward Marland for emphasis. "If I would have known your men were going to be stepping on my boys' heels, this whole thing might have turned out better."

Marland's eyes smoldered within their sockets, burning through the cold and snow that stood between himself and the Major. "You'd best point that finger somewhere else, boy."

"Or what? It looks to me like your men have found something better to do this evening."

"Then you'd best look again."

Major Waterman did just that, if only to make light of the fact that the lot was empty except for himself, his men and Marland. As he looked around the darkened lot, however, he noticed bits of shadow moving all around the perimeter.

Some were close to the ground and others were up on nearby rooftops, but they were all making their presence known the instant Waterman looked at them. There were nine total. All of Marland's surviving men were present and accounted for.

"Very efficient," Waterman said, unable to hide just how impressed he truly was. "And with all these men trained so very well, remind me how they dealt with Adams."

"That's what we're here to decide. And even though I promise to hear you out, I swear I will take this little venture away from you the moment I don't think you can handle it. This is your last chance to impress me, Waterman. If you don't, I'll cut you out of this whole thing entirely." Shifting so that he was once again staring rigidly out into the night, Marland added, "None of this will affect your finder's fee, of course."

It was all Waterman could do to keep from snapping when he heard those words. A finder's fee was a slap in the face considering just how much work he'd put into this. Not only did he get word of what Peter Banks was working on, he acted quickly enough to send one of his men to kill the army's messenger before he sent a report detailing the Englishman's plan to fulfill his contract.

As far as the army was concerned, Banks had yet to accept the offer, which freed the Major to take it over for himself. If it wasn't for Marland's connections to the military as well as other mercenary outfits, Waterman would have been able to deal with the weapon himself.

But since he didn't know the right people to approach with such a major commodity as Peter's revolutionary weapon, Waterman would have had to accept something less than what the gun was truly worth. Looking back on it, taking a cut in pay would have been worth not having to deal with the likes of Marland. But it was too late for regrets. The time had come for the final hand to be dealt.

"Since we're all here," Waterman said, stepping forward and turning to address everyone in the lot, seen or unseen. "I guess we might as well get started. I'll make this short and sweet, gentlemen. We all know the gun is finished and fully functional. That means it's time for us to—"

Marland stopped him with a quickly raised hand. When the Major was looking, Marland used that hand to point up to one of the men positioned on the rooftop. "Someone's coming," he said.

"Pardon me," came a voice from the direction Marland had been pointing. "But we all weren't here." Clint stepped forward with Peter following him. "Now we are. Please, Major, fill me in on this plan of yours."

FORTY-FIVE

Major Waterman stared at Clint for a full second before he looked over to the men beside him and said, "Kill that son of a bitch!"

Bill was the first to go for his gun, but the other two of Waterman's men weren't far behind. All three men had been itching for this moment to come and had only been waiting for the order to be given. The sound of them clearing leather was followed by the sound of shots being loosed one after another.

Lead hissed through the air like angry hornets and slapped into flesh and bone. The man standing closest to Waterman snapped back as though he'd been punched by an invisible fist, blood spraying from the fresh hole in his skull.

Bill caught a round in the chest, which staggered him back a few steps as the man beside him dropped over dead.

After that, there was only silence.

Smoke drifted through the air, stirred up by the passing cold breeze. At the center of that smoke stood Clint Adams. The Colt filled his right hand and was already pointing back in Bill's direction. Not a single one of the men in that lot had seen the Colt move from its spot at Clint's side. One second it had been holstered, and the next it was spitting death at the last of Waterman's killers.

Bill started to say something as he lifted his gun to shoot. The last of his energy left him before he could pull the trigger, and he fell heavily to the ground.

"That was a fine display, Mister Adams," Marland said. "Now have your friend hand over that weapon."

"That's not going to happen," Clint answered.

Marland shook his head slowly. "I've already been disappointed too many times since I've been here. Don't do it again by showing me that you are so much dumber than you look."

Another shot cracked the night, kicking up a gout of dirty snow at Clint's feet.

"The next shot could very well put you down, Mister Adams," Marland pointed out. "And believe me when I say that I've got more men than even you can handle. We have the high ground and killing you would be no problem. The only reason I haven't already is because I know you just happened to stumble into this. Drop the pistol."

Clint looked around, quickly seeing that there were at least half a dozen guns trained on him and Peter. "And if we do? What then?"

"Then you best get out of my town," Waterman said. "We don't give a shit what you do after that."

Clint looked over his shoulder to Peter, tossed the Colt and nodded. The Englishman reached inside his coat and removed the awkward crankgun. Even though the weapon wasn't strapped to his arm, several of Marland's men shifted their aim to cover him.

"Clint?" Peter asked hesitantly. "Are you sure about this?"

"We don't have a choice," Clint answered. "Hand it over or we won't walk away from this spot." Lowering his voice and meeting Peter's eyes, he added, "I'm sorry, old friend."

Peter walked slowly across the lot and up to Major Waterman. He held out the weapon as though he was handing over his only child and turned his back quickly when it was taken from him.

"This ends here," Clint said. "Let Peter walk away now and don't bother him again."

"Fine by me," Marland said. "I'm done with him anyway." Once again, Marland lifted a finger toward a nearby rooftop. Once again, a shot came from there. Only this time, the bullet didn't punch into the ground, but into the chest of Peter Banks.

The Englishman was knocked off his feet and landed heavily onto the cold earth.

Waterman stepped forward with a murderous glint in his eyes. "And for you, Gunsmith, let's see if you're faster than this."

Waterman took hold of the crank-gun around the handle, sliding his fingers around the grip and pointing it at Clint. Grabbing onto the crank handle which protruded from the side, he started turning it as though he was working a drill.

The barrels turned around once without firing until the first round was dropped into place. Waterman was still smiling when the first round went off and sent a blast of sparks from the mechanism.

Clint detected a faint metallic clang right before the next round went off. He knew that was the sound of the gun breaking and the ammunition jamming in the barrel, which was just what he'd wanted to happen when he'd asked Peter to make the special modifications. Even when he'd assigned the project to Banks, Clint didn't imagine the backfire would be so spectacular.

The crank-gun exploded in a blast of fire and metal shards. Since Peter had filled the barrels so they couldn't fire, the bulk of the eruption blew in the opposite direction, turning Waterman's face and upper chest into a mess of shredded meat and bone.

Waterman's body dropped. All that remained of the crank-gun was a twisted knot of warped, scorched metal.

Clint stood his ground and turned to look at Marland.

For a moment, the mercenary had turned back into that silent statue that he'd resembled before. Finally, after the last echoes of the backfire had faded, he said, "There isn't anything left in the workshop, is there?"

Clint shook his head. "Nope. But you can look all you want."

After staring at Peter's unmoving body, he snapped his fingers and all of the men around him faded back into the darkness. "Cross my path again, Adams, and I'll have you shot on sight."

With that said, Marland turned and walked away.

"Are they gone?"

Clint was sitting in the same stable where Eclipse had been waiting for him during his entire stay in Gemmell. "Hell yeah, they're gone. There's no reason for any of those hired guns to stay around. Besides," he added, offering a hand to Peter Banks, "the only man who can put that gun back together is dead."

Peter got up and pulled open his coat. The second project he'd been working on was a pair of metal plates held together with short lengths of rope. The heavy piece hung on his shoulders, covering his chest and back. It took some effort getting it off and when he finally dropped it to the ground, he stared at the blackened dent where that bullet had hit.

"I swear I thought they were onto us," Peter said. "But they couldn't see me breathing with this covering me. It's so bloody heavy that I must have dropped like dead weight."

"I'll say it's heavy," Clint replied. "I was the one that had to drag your carcass all the way back here just in case someone was watching."

"And you're sure they're gone?"

"I'm sure. I spotted them all before we walked into that lot and I spotted them all creeping away not too long ago. Like I said, there's no reason for them to stay. That is, after they ransack every last inch of your workshop."

Peter swore under his breath. "I guess that's the way it must be. I can start over somewhere else. Thanks to you, Clint. I never would have thought I could get out of this. Thank you so much."

"No problem. Get in touch with me after you settle into your new place, which better be far away from here."

"It will be, I assure you. But tell me, how did you know this bulletproofing would do the trick?"

"I got to know Waterman well enough playing cards with the man. He's a cheat and a liar, but he's smart enough to cover all the angles. He would have shot you if that other one hadn't."

"And he would have shot me in the back, right? I mean, that's how you knew you could put me out there and I would be all right?"

"They had to see you dead, Peter. You know that. Otherwise, they would have been after you for the rest of your life to make more guns like that."

"And you knew they would have shot me in the back. Either that or in the heart. Otherwise, they could have shot me in the head and I would have been dead for real." Peter was obviously getting more than a little uncomfortable the more he thought about what had happened. "You knew they'd shoot me in the back or heart, right?"

That devil's spark was back, only this time it wasn't in Peter's eyes. It was in Clint's as he answered, "No, but I was betting that you wouldn't worry about that until after this was all over."

Watch for

EMPTY HAND

263rd novel in the exciting GUNSMITH series
from Jove

Coming in November!

J. R. ROBERTS
THE
GUNSMITH

JAKE LOGAN
TODAY'S HOTTEST ACTION WESTERN!

Explore the exciting Old West with one of the men who made it wild!

**AVAILABLE WHEREVER BOOKS ARE SOLD OR
TO ORDER CALL:**

1-800-788-6262

(Ad # B112)